THE
ANCHOR
IN THE
OVAL

HARRISON BLACK

THE
ANCHOR
IN THE
OVAL

Archway Publishing books may be ordered through booksellers or by contacting:

Archway Publishing
1663 Liberty Drive
Bloomington, IN 47403
www.archwaypublishing.com
1 (888) 242-5904

ISBN: 978-1-4808-7067-3 (sc)
ISBN: 978-1-4808-7065-9 (hc)
ISBN: 978-1-4808-7066-6 (e)

Library of Congress Control Number: 2018914120

Print information available on the last page.

Archway Publishing rev. date: 01/14/2019

For my grandsons
Matthew and Ryan
honor thy family, honor thy selves

CHAPTER ONE

Colony of New Jersey 1775

T HE MERCHANT SHIP *Clara* threw its ropes to the dock and was finally tied off. It had taken weeks to cross the Atlantic, and both crew and passenger were relieved. The wealthier passengers departed first followed by servants and trunks. Then the unloading of the holds started with the ropes and pulleys as the goods from England were to be sold to the populace. When the cargo was done, the human hold was open. The indentured servants from England had been packed into dark spaces. The conditions were terrible, but the Captain looked on and counted heads. From Portsmouth he had taken on 56 souls, and today he watched as 48 walked ashore. He considered this a success. Some were families, most were single men who had been judged in a British court and sentenced

to time in the Colonies. These people were already
bought and paid for. Their "employers" lined the dock
to take charge of them, for this was the high quality
worker force needed on the farms or in the city mills.
He heard his name called out and walked over to a
man who told him to join a group in front of the red
building. He was tired from the trip, and he stank
from the close quarters living. There were five of them,
all men, and they were told to jump up onto a wagon.
The man who called his name got into the front seat
and took the reins. The two horses took off in slow
trot. This new country was not like England, it was
open and green, the air smelled better. He could see
the town disappear and soon they were in open country. Trees and streams appeared as the wagon continued down a curving dirt road. He soon fell asleep
for what seemed a long time, was cut short when the
wagon stopped. They had arrived at a farm with a large
house, and barn. Told to get out of the wagon they
stood in line as the owner exited the house.

"You are in the King's Colony of New Jersey. My
name is Abraham Bishop and I have purchased your
debt from the court. You will work on this farm, until
my purchase has been paid off, then you are free to
leave. I will provide you with shelter, food, clothing, and the tools you need to do your jobs. We grow
tomatoes, squash, green beans, melons, apples and

cabbage. We have four dairy cows, a herd of pigs, cattle and chickens. We sell everything we produce. My son Caleb is the field boss, and all orders will come from him. Do your job correctly, listen to direction, do not consider escape, you will be tracked down and punished. Does everybody understand?"

The group nodded yes. Caleb took over and told them to follow him to a pond. They were told to strip off all their clothes and shoes. Each was handed a bar of soap and told to jump in and clean them selves off. The water was cold, but refreshing. He drank some and his thirst was quenched. They all were ordered to get out of the pond and follow Caleb to the main barn. Inside were other men handing them new clothing and boots. The clothes were new; the boots were leather with strings that you tied to keep the boot on your feet. Everyone got a straw hat, and a blanket. Following Caleb they left the barn and were taken to several small buildings where they found beds with soft hay mattresses. Caleb told them to get settled and when they heard the dinner bell come to the big table outside the barn. Tomorrow they would work. William Conway was anxious to start a new life.

CHAPTER TWO

Shrewsbury, NJ 1791

CONWAY WAS NOW 35 years old. In England he had been a miller of grain, his business small but enough to survive. He had taken a loan from a man, and was unable to pay it back in time. Sentenced to debtors' prison he rotted for a year, then his sentence was bought for indentured servitude. He had spent the last fifteen years on Bishop's farm and now had worked off his debt. During this period a war was being fought all around him. The former Royal colony of New Jersey was now a part of a new nation called America, and William was now eager to forge his future. The time he spent, he had learned all there was to know about farming, for he was a quick learner, and would now put that knowledge to work. Leaving the Bishop plantation he had about eight pounds in his pocket. He had heard that the Jersey coast offered some opportunity, so with a sack on his back he walked south. In Thimbletown he signed on as crew on a fishing boat. The work was hard and dangerous, but he picked up the skills and soon progressed to second mate. For the next three years he worked as a fisherman, then one day in Philadelphia he signed on with a large merchant ship bound for Europe. He visited France, Spain and Italy, but never would set foot in England. He again worked himself up on the boat, becoming first mate, then third officer. He learned to navigate by the stars, and soon knew how to plot a course. When he was 45, the group owners of the merchant fleet wanted him to captain a ship, he now would get a share of the cargo sales. For the next two years his reputation grew as a steady man in a storm, and a man who could bring his cargo in on time. He married a Jersey girl from Elizabeth and bought a home in Waretown. He made sure he had the land to go with the house and hired farmers to make the land profitable. After several years of sailing the oceans, he left the sea, and returned to his family. Now in his fifties with a wife and two young children he began to enjoy life. With money he bought more farmland, and soon his Waretown farm was one of the biggest in the state. With markets in Philadelphia, New Brunswick, Elizabeth and New York the William Conway Company prospered. In 1809 a flu epidemic claimed his beloved wife, and he became a different man. With two sons to raise, he started to invest in various ventures, most of them failures. Within time he had lost his company and farm. He had known the scourge of poverty, and with his last money he moved his family to Heislerville on the Delaware Bay, there he bought an oyster boat. With his sons they soon were making money in the oyster trade. As his sons matured they learned all from their father about the sea. In 1833 a hurricane hit the NJ coast, William Conway was killed as his boat capsized and sunk. He was the last honest Conway. The future of the Conway family did not stay with farming oysters, it took a turn when the oldest son Benjamin saw the lucrative side of smuggling. It began when he was out in his boat and came across the wreckage of a merchant ship. Strewn amongst the rocks and beach were the cargo items. He anchored and began going thru the rubble. Finding sealed chests, and huge trunks he determined he had a small fortune. A few weeks later it returned some two thousand dollars in the Philadelphia market. Convincing his brother Thomas, to join him, they plied the nearby coast and were disappointed in finding nothing. Benjamin Conway knew he could make a lot of money if he had a plan. He looked at navigation maps and realized that they were in the middle of some of the biggest navigation hazards along the coast.

Could he utilize these hazards to their advantage? It was Thomas who came forth with an idea. They knew when storms were coming, and they knew the location of the Federal lighthouses. What if they simulated a light where there was none, could they lure a ship onto the rocks? Crew abandons ship, cargo is strewn all over for easy pickings. They would collect under the salvage law and sell for a hefty profit. Benjamin like the idea, and on November 23, 1841 a serious storm came up the Jersey coast. The brothers were on a cliff off of Townsend's Inlet. With an ox and a contraption made of wood holding 4 large oval sea lanterns, they walked the ox back and forth on a small path above the ocean. To a ship on the stormy ocean and with the rain acting like a screen, those lights could have looked like the light at Barnegat. All the maps said once past the Barnegat light a vessel could move safely to port. However, moving to port once passing the ox light spelled doom. From their cliff side position, the brothers heard the ship hitting the rocks. At dawn they found their treasure trove and gathered their booty. With violent sea storms averaging some 5 to 6 a year the Conway's prospered. The brothers would father some six sons and as the years went by it was a profitable family affair. The daughters married and became the Blaine and Thompson faction. The family grew rich again, but with the guidance left by William Conway, they invested in land. Farms sprung up, dairy cattle and beef cattle herds added more to their wealth. And with wealth came power, political power. The next Conway generation became the power brokers of South Jersey. Their money and backing assured one the office. They had judges in their pocket, Washington congressmen and senators at their whim. It was also a time for the next generation's children to become educated and sociably acceptable. In 1886 William Conway III graduated from Princeton. The next year Alvin William Conway graduated the US Naval Academy. In 1890 Frederick Conway Thompson graduated Harvard. Soon they all married into the highest of America's society. From an indentured servant came forth the American dream. Yet, the family core businesses, smuggling always remained vibrant and profitable. 1907 the youngest son of Albert Conway, Roger, became the head of the family business. Roger's first act was to change the name from The Conway Company to Seaford Incorporated. He changed direction from causing ships to wreck to having his own ships smuggle in contraband goods to a network of secret coves and dock warehouses. Long before prohibition he brought in Irish and Scottish liquors as well as French fragrances, Turkish rugs, and African Ivory, all tax-free. The few who counted, knew of him and Seaford Inc. became the go to supplier of the exotic and illegal. In 1917 with Europe at War his newly opened Asian connections supplied him heroin. Up and down the Jersey coast the Seaford ships plied their trade, making the Conway's one of America's secretly wealthy families. Surrounded by his brother's, and first cousins Roger was no stranger to crime. Anyone who raised his hand and tried to compete with Seaford was dealt with harshly and with dispatch. People disappeared; bodies were found in swamps or floating in the ocean. Roger was feared, and he in turn demanded loyalty. At one family meeting he stood up and rolled up his left sleeve to display a tattoo on his inner arm. It was a simple sea anchor enclosed in an oval border.

"This is our heritage. The anchor represents the sea and the oval border represents the oval glass lanterns that were carried by the ox. No matter if you're a Conway, Blaine or Thompson we are family. If you are with me, then show it."

All present in the next few days were tattooed, even the high society Conway's'. When Prohibition became the law of the land, Seaford Inc. was already ahead of the curve. Roger had culminated deals with the gangsters and bootleggers to be their main supplier. Cash up front at time of sale was the edict. If someone shortchanged him, he was dealt with instantly for an agreement was an agreement.

THREE

1968 South Bronx

THE CORNER OF Brown Place and Monsignor Ryan Blvd. was a supermarket. You didn't buy groceries for your house; you purchased heroin, crack cocaine, and marijuana. It was like a McDonald's Drive-thru, you lined up on Brown Place, someone would come to your car and you would tell him what you wanted. A series of hand signals started the order process. They would tell you to pay a certain guy with a certain colored woolen cap. You would move your car up, and that guy with the right colored cap would be at your window. He would take your money, and tell you to look for guy in a particular sport jacket. If in your case you needed heroin look for the guy in the Jet's jacket, the Giants jacket was for cocaine and crack, while the Mets jacket was for marijuana . Move up your car again and a guy in right sports jacket would appear. He looked at you, then pointed to a guy standing at your passengers window. Down came your window and he threw your order on the seat. You now could leave the neighborhood. This went on 24 hours a day, 7 days a week, except they closed on Christmas Day. All types were in the Brook Place line from junkies in taxicabs to Bentley's from Great Neck. The proprietors of this illegal goldmine were a Hispanic gang called the 135th Street Toros. The Toros were led by Jaime Ordonez, 34 years old with tattooed tears falling from his eyes, Jaime took in some $2 million dollars a week. The Toros under his leadership were once a neighborhood nothing, today they were powerful and wealthy. They had resisted takeovers from rivals, told the Mafia to take a hike and were not beholding to anyone because Jaime had done his homework. He had learned that success was to have your own supply and sell it. His product came from his home city in the Dominican Republic, Bonao. His family provided the product and final transport to Brown Place. On a fall morning at about 2AM a Mercedes driven by a red-haired yuppie is in line. The driver had been high on coke since the morning. He orders crack and goes through the process, but when the crack is delivered he gets into an argument with the seller. He jumps out of his car and draws a gun. Within a second, eight guns are sighted in on this crazy white guy. He demands more crack for the money he spent and claims they cheated him. A man wearing a fur jacket comes out of doorway with his hands in the air telling the white guy to lower his weapon, but the red headed guy keeps yelling he wants what he paid for. With his hands still in the air, the man tries to reason with him, and moves closer. For no reason, the white guy unloads his gun into the man with his arms still raised. Responding the eight guns shoot the red-headed man, he is spun around like a top finally falling to the street. There is total silence as figures fill the street. They pick up the man with the fur jacket and bring him into a building. Others remove the gun from the dead man, while another grabs the crack from the front seat. Another two men open the trunk of the Mercedes and throw in the dead red- headed shooter, while another gets in to the car and drives it away. Within a minute of the shooting, Brown Place is back to normal as two customer cars line up on the street. Inside the building, the body is carefully laid down and a call is made to Jaime.

"Hello"

"Jefe, we had a problem a gringo went crazy, he pulled a gun and killed Ramon."

Silence

"Where is my brother now?"

"He's in Candida's apartment."

More silence

"Is he presentable for burial?"

"No Jefe, his face and head were hit, I am sorry."

"Call Armendez, the undertaker and have him pick up the body. Tell him to make my brother presentable for his mother. Where is this bastardo gringo?"

"He's is dead, we put him in his trunk, and Juanito has driven it to the river."

"Now I must call Bonao and tell my mother her baby son is dead. Goodnight Guillermo."

"Goodnight my Jefe."

CHAPTER FOUR

1968 Philadelphia
650 Broad Street, Philadelphia
The law offices of Conway, Stoddard and Daniels

VINCENT CONWAY TOOK the call in his office. His wife Monica was distraught.

"Yes Monica, what is it?"

"Junior has disappeared. He is not at home, did not show up at the New York office, his girlfriend last saw him 2 days ago. They were to go to a party tonight. I'm worried he may be in trouble Vince."

"He may be on one his escapades, you know him."

"No Vince, not this time. You need to find him."

"Alright, I will see what I can do."

His next call was to a number he knew by heart.

"Cousin Vincent, been awhile."

"Hello Reggie, I got a problem, need some family help."

He proceeded to tell about junior's disappearance, and what he knew about his son.

"We'll get on it right away, Vince. I will call you when we find him."

"Thank you Reggie."

As he hung up the phone, Vincent Conway put both his hands on his head and felt a headache coming on. As his left sleeve rolled down he saw the tattoo on his arm, the oval around the anchor. This curse on his arm had made him rich beyond his wildest expectations, yet he knew the future implications, and how fragile was ones control of life. His father had urged him to become an attorney and represent the interests of the family Conway. As head legal counsel for the Seaford Corporation he prospered financially and personally. A director of Philadelphia's Union Club, University of Pennsylvania trustee, and club memberships at both Merion and Pine Valley he enjoyed the stature. Reality was he knew where all the Seaford skeletons were buried and where the money was located and when it was moved. In the family Vincent was well respected, and his personal honor was carried like a shield. He had wished his oldest son, Vincent Jr., had the felt the same way, but instead had run his life on a winding road of self-destruction. Now his wife feared for her child, and he had no choice but to reach to the family for help. Cousin Reggie Conway had inherited the mantle of Seaford Inc. from his father Roger. Roger had been a stern teacher to the son. Reggie had learned and earned his position through fear, pain and perseverance. He had killed for the family and his reputation for ruthlessness was legendary. As head of the Clan he decided the present and future status of every member. Those that displayed an aptitude at running a business benefitting the interests of the family were financially backed. College educations were paid for, and the graduate was guaranteed a job and employed. Those not possessing college material were employed doing the yeoman work. It was important to Reggie that the family continues to flourish and remain strong. When Vincent called, it was his duty to place all the resources available in finding a lost son.

CHAPTER FIVE

1968
Farmingdale, NY

T HE DAMN BEEPER awoke Morris "Red" Blackman. He looked at the clock it was 5AM. He knew who would beep him so early, his partner Sean Feeney. Rubbing his red haired head he dialed the number.

"What do you want?"

"LT gave us a case, get dressed you lazy bastard and meet me at the end of Soundview Avenue by the water."

"OK, give me a few minutes to get dressed."

"What do you think your going to, a formal event?"

"You're such an Irish asshole."

Then he hung up. He was in his 17th year as a NYPD Detective, First Grade. He and Feeney had been partners for over ten years. They were the best team in the Bronx for they closed cases, and that is what the brass wanted. Known as "Bagels and Beer", the Jew and the Irishman had amassed a record of solved cases and good convictions. In 1959 as young beat officers they came across a bank robbery in progress. There was a shootout, three of the four robbers were killed and the leader wounded. Blackman and Feeney were given their Detective shields and assigned to the South Bronx as third grade detectives in the 41st Precinct. In 1962 they tracked down and captured the Cross Bronx Expressway sniper who had killed seven and terrorized the city for some ten months. It was Blackman who surmised the perpetrator frequented gun shows and may be ex-military. The investigation was lengthy and strenuous that eventually led them to a far right group in Dutchess County. Surveillances and checks uncovered the individual, and he was caught in the act of attempting to kill his eight victim. Blackman and Feeney both moved up the Detective grade ladder and continued to cement their notoriety. Blackman lived on Long Island with his wife and children; Feeney had just divorced for the third time and lived in Rockland County. As Blackman reached the end of Soundview Avenue, he saw Feeney standing with a cup of coffee looking at the water. Police divers were attaching cables to a sunken automobile. As the divers surfaced they gave the signal to haul it up. The tow truck winch strained, then starting gathering cable as the water logged car was brought up to the road. Blackman noticed it was a black Mercedes, maybe a year old. Feeney had the Emergency Service Unit team pry open the doors so the water could flow out. No one was in the car. Feeney saw at least 6 bullet holes in the driver's side door. Blackman motioned for the ESU to open the trunk. It popped and they saw the body. Putting on their latex gloves they felt around the body and under it, finding nothing.

Feeney said to a Patrolman,

"Call in the ME. "

As they waited they decided to search the car. Blackman took the front while Feeney checked the back. License plates were missing, the glove compartment and center console were empty. An empty package of Newport cigarettes was on the driver's side floor. Feeney had ripped off the back seat and found a used condom, he placed that in an evidence bag. The detectives were known by the arriving ME.

"Oh no, another Bagels and Beer case."

"Did your mother ever tell you not to be a doctor?" said Blackman.

"Matter of fact, she wanted me to be an accountant.

"Well Doctor, do your thing."

The ME checked the body and took the liver temperature.

"This guy is filled with bullets, and he has been marinating for awhile. Will be able to tell you more after the autopsy. With your permission?"

Blackman nodded yes and the body was put in a black body bag and placed in the morgue wagon.

Blackman questioned the reporting officer, a young kid who had just finished his second year.

"What's your name kid?"

"Patrolman Adam Wright, sir."

"How did you know that there was a car underwater?"

"My partner Patrolman Jason Tozzi and I patrol by here everyday. A guy who fishes regular down here, he waved us down. He said he could see a car underwater, so we called it in."

"About what time did he wave you down?"

"It was around 2AM."

"How did he see it? It is dark as ink down there."

"A passing tug and barge came by and their lights must have reflected off the car, that's what he said."

"Alright, thank you Officer Wright."

"Yes, Sir"

Blackman looked at Feeney,

"Sean, there was nothing in that car to identify him. Could be a mob hit?"

"Red, to many bullets. The mob guys are two shots to the back of the head, and usually twenty-two caliber.

Those holes were a lot bigger."

"Yeah, something not normal about this one. Anyway get the VIN number off the dash before they tow it to impound, maybe we can find out who owns it."

It now was almost 8AM, and they needed to eat breakfast.

"Sean, breakfast is on me, as long as you stay under $6 bucks."

Feeney just smiled and they both left the scene for the cozy diner they both enjoyed.

# CHAPTER SIX

1968
Bronx County Medical Examiner Office
2455 Pelham Parkway

MEDICAL EXAMINER DR. Lawrence Shapiro had finished suturing up the chest cavity, when Blackman and Feeney arrived.

Blackman,

"What do you have Doc?"

"Well let us begin with the head. I found one bullet that was embedded in the brain, looks like a 9mm. This was not the kill shot. In his mouth in the lower jaw were two bullets, one a 9mm the other a .45. These did not kill him. Oh yes, the victim had very expensive dental work, his upper teeth were all porcelain capped. One bullet to the throat, another 9mm, from his neck down to his waist he had seven different bullet holes.

This 357 Mag bullet was the kill shot; it was dead center in his heart. The other six bullets were; one-357 Mag, three- 9mm, and two-.45. From his waist down he had another twelve holes, five passed thru his body, three all 9mm were in his left leg. One-.45 in his left foot, One- .308 rifle bullet in his left thigh, and finally two-.38 Specials in his right knee. This guy smoked a lot, and you could see the beginnings of lung cancer. He was a crack user. We found it in his blood levels. His fingernails were recently manicured. There is a birthmark on his inner thigh. He has a tattoo on the inside of his left arm. We fingerprinted him and should be getting back the results this afternoon. His clothing was expensive designer brands, and he wore high priced handmade Italian slip-ons. I will forward everything we have to Forensics."

"Doc can you take a photo of that tattoo?"

"Sure, I send it down to your precinct."

"Thanks Doc."

As they left the ME offices, Feeney said to Blackman,

"That was a lot of bullets for just one guy, must have really pissed someone off."

"No, he pissed several people off."

Arriving back at the precinct, they headed up to the second floor detective rooms. As they passed the lieutenant, they were both summoned to come inside.

Detective Lt. Washington Lewis was a big man. His voice was booming, and when he called your name, you knew it.

"Red, what do have on the victim from the river?"

"Nothing concrete. Waiting for the prints to come back, and have a request in on the car's VIN. Other than the fact this guy wore expensive clothes, and had good dental work, we have no reason to believe why a group of people filled him with lead. That car was stripped of anything that could identify the victim, and was driven to be dumped in the river. Where the shooting happened, your guess is a good as mine. We're going to have to hit the streets for information, and narcotics will have to help us get it."

"OK, keep me in the loop."

"Will do LT."

At their desks, Feeney found an envelope addressed to him. It contained the VIN results.

> New York Department of Motor Vehicles confirms VIN 7BVR4589TWW-23995ZHQP34581 Is a 1968 Mercedes 300SDL manufactured Wiesbaden, Germany 1988. Distributed to Mercedes North America and delivered to dealer Midtown Mercedes, 1492 Avenue of the Americas, NYC. Registered to Conway,

Stoddard and Daniels 650 Broad Street, Philadelphia, PA. Licensee Audra McClellan.

Sounds like a law firm. As in all inquiries you get a hold of the local police jurisdiction. Feeney had the number listed and placed the call.

"Philadelphia Police Department, how can I connect your call?"

"Homicide please."

A few seconds went by, and it was answered.

"Homicide, Detective Sergeant Yardley."

"Detective Sergeant, this is Detective 1st Grade Sean Feeney from the NYPD, I will require a death notification."

"Ok, give me a name and the address."

"All we were able to identify was a car with a VIN. Still waiting fingerprints on the victim. Car was registered to Conway, Stoddard and Daniels, 650 Broad Street, Philadelphia. VIN 7BVR4589TWW23995HQP34581 is a 1968 Black Mercedes. Licensee Audra McClellan."

"So you want us to verify who the car belongs to and who may have been driving it?"

"Yes".

"Alright, we will get on it. Can the next of kin get in touch with someone?"

"Yes, call me at 212-477-2810."

"Ok, Detective Feeney will do."

"Thanks."

Feeney looked at Blackman and said,

"Philly PD will get to the address from the VIN, and hopefully someone will get back to us.

"Good, you know this case is more narcotics than a mere murder, somebody has got to know something. What was the name of the Sergeant and his team out of Bronx South?"

"Puerto Rican name, started with a V, let me think, yeah Velasquez."

"That's it, thanks, your good for something."

Blackman dialed Bronx South and asked for Sgt. Pete Velasquez."

"Hello, Valasquez."

"Sarge, this is Detective Blackman, four-one squad.

We have a homicide that was fished out of the river, completely devoid of identification, except for the car VIN. White male, expensive car, expensive clothes, autopsy showed he used crack. He died from a gunshot to the heart, accompanied by some other twenty plus bullets throughout his body. Could use some help on this, especially from the "street telegraph", so if your guys hear anything let me know.

"You know if this guy was here for drugs, and he did something like try and pull a scam, or pull a gun on these dealers, these drug gangs would kill him. So many bullets that tells me he may have killed one of them, and they got their revenge. Yeah, I'll get the word out, something like this doesn't go unnoticed."

"Thanks, Sarge."

"Sean, Velasquez says if someone tried to scam or pulls a gun the dealers will shoot back, and if he kills one of them, he'll get the broadside, like our victim."

"Either our guy was out of his mind, or just plain unaware of the street rules around here, doesn't matter he's dead, and we still have to solve it."

 SEVEN

1968
Offices of Conway, Stoddard and Daniels

"ARE YOU AUDRA McClellan?"
"Yes, what can I do for you officer?

"We have an inquiry from the New York City Police Department regarding a car found in one of their investigations. Records show the car is owned by this firm."

"This firm has some thirty registered cars. Do you have a make and VIN?"

He handed her the information, and she went to a book self and removed a ledger. She found the name and did not show any concern, for she never liked or trusted Vinny Conway Junior. In her twenty years with the firm she knew she had to get permission to release the information.

"Officer I have to get a partner to write off on this one, can you wait here?"

"Yes, ma 'me."

She got on the elevator and took it up to the next floor.

Walking down to the last office, she knocked twice, a voice said enter.

"Audra, how are you? What can I do for you?"

"Mr. Conway, I have a Philadelphia Police Detective downstairs with an inquiry from the New York Police. It is in regard to one of the firm's car being involved in a police investigation."

"Is there a problem?"

"The vehicle was assigned to Vincent Jr."

Conway became very quiet, and gathered his thoughts.

"Audra, please bring the Detective here."

'Yes, Mr. Conway."

Four minutes later, the officer was in front of Conway.

"Detective, what is all this about?"

"NYPD called to find out who owned the car, we were asked to verify and inquire who was assigned the car. When we verified the driver, I am to give you this number to call."

"Well I am the next of kin, and you can give me that number."

"With all respect sir, I will need the name of that assigned driver."

Conway was silent for a second, then looked at the detective,

"That car was assigned to my son Vincent Conway Jr., I will take that number now."

He quietly thought for a minute, then made the phone call

"Yes, this is Detective Feeney."

"Detective, my name is Vincent Conway Sr.. I am told your have an investigation regarding a car owned by our firm and assigned to my son Vincent Conway Jr."

"Yes, Mr. Conway we have an investigation involving that vehicle found in the East River and an unidentified male body that was in the trunk. We are awaiting a fingerprint check to return an identification of the body.

"Sir, if you think this may be your son, then we need the body identified and confirmed at our Medical Examiners Office."

"I know the procedures. I would appreciate a time to meet you and view the deceased."

"Mr. Conway that would be most helpful in our investigation. Shall we meet tomorrow at 1PM at 2455 Pelham Parkway, Bronx."

"Yes, I will be there. Thank you Detective Feeney."

'Thank you, Mr. Conway."

CHAPTER EIGHT

1968
Seaford Incorporated Offices, Strathmere, NJ

REGGIE CONWAY SAW the incoming call from Vincent, "Yes, Vincent."

"I will be going to the Bronx tomorrow to identify a body. My heart says it may be my son Vinny. The NYPD found the car in the river, and the body was in the trunk. They have yet to identify the body, awaiting fingerprints. What do you want me to do?"

"Vincent, go and identify the body. If it is Vinny Jr. then confirm it. Get as much information on what they believe happened, and get back to me. Meanwhile, we need to clean his apartment, so nothing comes back to haunt us. Send me his address and I'll get it done within two hours. You stay calm cousin, if it is Vinny

Jr, the family will take care of it. Now our hearts are with you and Monica. Goodbye cousin."

Reggie knew what to do and how to react. He had been well trained and groomed by his father. At sixteen he had killed his first man, and had earned the tattoo. His temper was legendary and his enemies stayed away from any Seaford enterprise. Even the mob crossed over to the other side when they knew Reggie was involved. In 1959, the Philadelphia mob tried to muscle in on Seaford's drug distribution network, they sent in a hit team of four to take down Reggie. Reggie killed them all, and had the bodies delivered to then family boss's estate in Bryn Mawr minus their heads. The mob got the message and from then on stayed clear. Someone now attacked a family member, one who wore the tattoo. Vengeance, sayeth the Book of Conway, will not go unheeded.

CHAPTER NINE

1968
1136 Park Avenue, Manhattan

THE DOORMAN KNEW the two men who entered the lobby; they were friends of Mr. Conway on the 10th Floor. They entered the elevator and were inside the apartment via the key they had been given. One started in the kitchen, while the other hit the bedroom. In the kitchen they found a loaded 9mm Glock. The bedroom bathroom yielded about four bags of crack, and in the nightstand was a full bag of grass. In the den they found a black book of addresses and phone numbers. In the dining room was another loaded pistol and a small safe in the hutch. These two knew how to open a safe. Inside they found papers with the Seaford Inc. letterhead and removed them. In the guest bedroom they found two more loaded pistols and a sawed-off twelve gauge shotgun. Satisfied they had taken all that was needed they left carrying a suitcase and golf bag. With a wave to the doorman they got into a van and made for the New Jersey shore.

CHAPTER TEN

1968
Bronx County Medical Examiners Office

WILLIAM CONWAY'S LIMOUSINE pulled up to the front of building, Conway waiting for his driver to open the door then exited and entered the building. In the lobby Feeney saw him coming and approached him.

"Mr. Conway?"

"Yes, are you Detective Feeney?"

"Yes, sir, and this is my partner Detective Blackman."

Conway extended his hand and nodded.

"If you will follow me to the identification room."

They all walked down a hallway, and Feeney opened a door for Conway, they all stepped inside. There was a window covered by a curtain, Feeney spoke into the intercom, and the curtain opened. As Conway viewed the body, he gasped. It was Vinny Jr. and he had been slaughtered. Conway, became lightheaded and had to sit. Blackman brought him a glass of water. Feeney asked,

"Mr. Conway, can you identify the deceased?"

"That is my son, Vincent Charles Conway, Jr.. Who could have done this to my boy?"

Feeney spoke in the intercom and the curtain closed.

"Sir, that's what we are trying to find out. Can you provide some information we do not have?"

Conway just nodded his head.

Blackman,

"I think it would be better if we move to a conference room down the hall."

In the conference, both detectives faced the father across a table.

"What was your son's birthplace and date of birth Mr. Conway?

"He was born in Sea Isle City, NJ on April 4, 1945."

"His mother's maiden name."

"Monica Glover."

"His last known address?"

"1136 Park Avenue, Manhattan."

"His occupation?"

"He was an attorney in the firm's New York City office."

"What law school did he attend?"

"Villanova Law, Philadelphia. Graduated two year ago."

"Did he live alone?"

"To my knowledge yes."

Blackman,

"Mr. Conway, did your son have any enemies?"

"None that I know."

"When was the last time you saw your son.?"

"About a month ago, my wife and I took him out for dinner in Philadelphia."

"How did he appear to you?"

"Same Junior, care free and happy."

Feeney,

"Mr. Conway do you have any idea why we found crack cocaine in your son's system?"

Conway went white, his mouth opened, but nothing came out.

"He had all the signs of steady usage, and it may be the reasons he was up here in the South Bronx."

"Oh my God, I had no idea. Your saying he may have been up there buying this poison? Who? Why would they kill him?"

Blackman,

"This is a photograph of a tattoo on your son's left forearm, did you ever see it before?

Conway looked at the photo. He had the same tattoo on his left arm.

"No, I never saw that before, he didn't have this past summer when we boated over to Bermuda."

Feeney;

"Mr. Conway, we are sorry for your loss, and have no more questions. Here is my card, please call if you have more information. The Medical Examiner Administrator will be in to talk to you about transferring the body for your funeral arrangements. Thank you for your time."

"Detectives, please find these animals."

Feeney,

"Yes, Sir."

About an hour later Conway place a call from his limousine.

"Reggie?"

"Yes, Vincent."

"My son is dead, they slaughtered him. He was in the South Bronx buying crack, and somebody killed him. He was put in the trunk and the car driven into the river. The cops asked me about his tattoo, I told them nothing. Find them Reggie kill them. Whatever it takes, money is no object."

"Vincent, you bear the family tattoo. The family

will find them and kill them, that is our right and legacy. Vincent, no more calls, when they are all dead, you will be notified."

"Thank you Reggie."

"My sincere condolences to you and Monica."

CHAPTER ELEVEN

1968
1136 Park Avenue, Manhattan

THEY HAD GOTTEN a search warrant for Conway's apartment. This apartment wreaked wealth, yet it gave them no clues. His closets were filled with expensive suits, and his wine rack likewise with high priced vintages. In his den, Feeney detected a smell and followed it to a drawer. In the rear of the drawer he uncovered a pistol cleaning kit, yet they had not found a gun. Blackman found a desk calendar for the year that was never used. It still bore the month of January page. Blackman thought, this guy was a lawyer, they usually jot down things. In his desk middle drawer was a NYC parking ticket. It was about 8 months old. Reading the ticket, it was for illegally parking in a loading zone in Brooklyn. Blackman saw the address was 156 Beard Street and the time of the ticket was 3:23AM. What was he doing down by the docks in Brooklyn, so early in the morning? Blackman put the ticket in an evidence bag. Feeney had come up with nothing, so this search hadn't yielded much on Conway's movements. As they left the elevator, the doorman stopped them.

"Look did anything happen to Mr. Conway, he is such a nice man."

"Yes, he was killed."

The doorman was shocked, he started to tear up, then pulled out handkerchief and wiped his eyes.

"Yesterday, his two friends came by, and left with a suitcase and a golf bag. They told me Mr. Conway called them to pick it up, and meet him at the airport."

Feeney.

"Well Mr. Conway was long dead. Do you remember the time they came in?"

"Yes, it was after my lunch. I'm back here from 12:30 PM till I leave at 5PM. I believe it was maybe about a little after 1PM."

Blackman looked around the lobby and saw two cameras.

"Do those cameras record everything in this lobby?"

"Yes, they do."

"Can we see the video from yesterday?"

"If you will follow me."

The doorman opened a door off the lobby and went down a stairwell that led to a lighted hallway. He opened another door and turn on the light. The room was a control center for the entire building. There were five active monitors. Blackman knew how to run the system.

"We can take it from here, I promise you if I break something the City of New York will pay for it."

The doorman was reluctant to leave, but he was not going to argue with two cops.

"Just turn off the lights when you leave, the door will lock behind you."

"Thanks."

Blackman got the lobby tape on rewind and stopped it at 12:55 PM. The doorman was on duty and there was plenty of activity with residents in and out as well as maintenance men carrying ladders. At 1:10PM two white males came into the lobby and waved to the doorman, who waved back. They waited for the elevator for about 30 seconds, and then entered. At 1:58PM they were observed exiting the elevator with one carrying a suitcase, the other a golf bag. Both were wearing hats that covered their features. With a wave to the doorman they were seen exiting. Blackman then found the exterior building camera, and rewound that to time of 1:55PM. At 1:59PM the two males were walking up Park Avenue, then went to the street where a black van was parked. Both got in through the side sliding door, and the van sped off. The license plate could not be seen.

Blackman looked at Feeney,

"Now that was not kosher. That was a professional team, and they cleaned that apartment."

"Jesus, Red, what the hell was that all about?"

"It looks like the former Mr. Conway had something more to hide, other than the fact he used crack. I think we're treading where someone doesn't want us to go."

CHAPTER TWELVE

1968
Seaford Inc.

REGGIE CONWAY HAD Vinny's little black address book. He knew that listed in here was either the name of the killer, or someone who could lead him to the killer. As he perused the names and addresses, he himself knew a few of these persons, for he had dealt with them in business. When he got to the L's, he saw the name Enrique Lordes. Known as Ricky, he and Reggie knew each other for over twenty-years. Ricky was a Manhattan drug dealer, and had bought heroin from Seaford. If anyone knew anything in New York it was Ricky Lourdes. Reggie called the number.

"Hello"

"Long time Ricky, this is Reggie Conway."

"Reggie how are you? It has been a long time. What can I do for you?"

"My cousin was fished out the East River with more than two dozen bullet holes. Who in the South Bronx is responsible for this Ricky? Find out for me, I want my vengeance."

Ricky knew the reputation of Reggie Conway and the long reach of Seaford, Inc., this was not a request you ignored.

"My condolences Reggie, I will find out who did it and get back to you personally."

"Thank you, my old friend."

Ricky hung up and left his office for his warehouse operation around the corner. He entered a room where his "street people" were sitting.

"Hey, everybody hit the streets and find about a white boy getting shot up in the South Bronx, he was fished from the river. Find out who is responsible and get back to me."

# CHAPTER THIRTEEN

1968
Four-One Precinct

BLACKMAN AND FEENEY had spread all the evidence all over the conference room table. The report of the used condom found under the seat of the victim's car, stated the DNA was not the same as the victims.

Blackman spoke,

"Maybe he was homosexual and had a session in the back seat."

Feeney

"Autopsy, says anal cavity showed no signs of abuse."

"Then he laid someone else in the backseat."

"Could be, but whatever happened, we have no other traces of somebody else being there."

"The tattoo on his left arm was not very old, wonder what it means?"

"No service record, so he wasn't in the Navy."

Blackman looked at the parking ticket and said to his partner.

"We got to go Brooklyn to the Seven-Six, and find the cop who wrote out this ticket."

Feeney.

"I'll drive, when you drive I get nervous."

From the South Bronx to the precinct in Brooklyn took about 50 minutes. Identifying them to the Desk Sergeant they asked for Officer W. Radwanski.

"He'll be coming thru that door in 30 minutes, his shift will be starting up."

"Okay, can you hold him for us, we be upstairs to call our boss."

"Sure, no problem."

They went up the center stairs to the Seven-Six Squad.

Looking around for some familiar faces, they spotted an old friend Sgt. Oliver Robbins hunched over a desk. Coming up behind him, Blackman said,

"You'd think they let this old relic retire."

Robbins spun around with a mad look on his face, then it turned to a smile when he saw Blackman and Feeney.

"Bagels and Beer, what the hell are you doing here?"

Everyone in the room looked up, for the duo's reputation was well known throughout the department.

Feeney,

"Ollie, just came down to check out a parking ticket."

Blackman,

"Yeah Ollie, we needed an excuse to come to Brooklyn.

How's the family and Rose?"

"Great, remember my youngest Hannah, she just had a little boy, that makes eight grandkids, Rose is enjoying them all."

Feeney,

"What do you hear from your son Matty."

"He made Lt. Colonel got his own battalion now at Fort Hood. He says they want to send him to Command and General School, must have bigger plans for him."

"That is good news. So when are you turning in the tin?"

"In three months I am done and out. Been everyplace they sent me, but when I was with you two, I can only smile. That was the most fun I had."

Another detective called for Blackman,

"Sarge has your guy waiting."

"Alright Ollie got to go, it was good seeing you."

"And you two characters just made me smile for the first time today."

They hugged and left for the downstairs desk.

"This is officer Walter Radwanski, Detectives."

They shook hands, and showed him the ticket.

"That was awhile ago, what do you need?"

"Can you show us the location, where the car was parked?"

"Sure, it's not far from here."

In about 10 minutes they were at the Brooklyn waterfront, a continuous wall of docks and buildings.

"If I remember it was right here in front of this building. See the no parking sign, well he was right here in front of the entrance."

They looked around for anything that might have looked where the driver may have gone, like a diner or a bar, there was nothing.

Blackman,

"Officer Radwanski, do streetwalkers frequent this area?"

"No, sir, they are all on the avenue six blocks over."

Feeney looked at Blackman and said,

"Nothing here, well at least we saw Ollie."

Blackman smiled, as he got back into the car, he saw

the nameplate on the building, Seaford Incorporated. It meant nothing to him at the time. Well another dead–end in this case he thought.

"Sean, let's get the officer back to the precinct, then we go back to the Bronx."

FOURTEEN

1968
Seaford Incorporated

REGGIE TOOK THE call.

"This is Ricky, that white boy killed the brother of the leader of the Toros during a drug deal. They opened up on him, and made him disappear."

"Who are the Toros?"

"The biggest Dominican drug gang in the city. Leader is Jaime Ordonez. They operate out of Brown Place in the South Bronx, got a bad reputation. That's all I got Reggie, need anything else?"

"No Ricky, you done good, I owe you."

After the call Reggie called in his oldest son Andrew.

Andrew was 28 years old, and a former Army Ranger Captain, who had the trust of his father.

"Andrew, here's the group that killed Vinny Conway Jr., pick your crew and clean them out, no mercy."

Andrew nodded to his father and left his office. Back in his office he called in his 2 younger brothers Freddie and Martin. They were identical twins both 26.

"This is the group that killed cousin Vincent, get the clan together, we meet in Red Hook tomorrow night at 8PM. Martin and me are heading up to the South Bronx to make a buy. Martin put some NY plates on the pickup, and Freddie you get the all the hardware together."

Within an hour Andrew and Martin were in a 1966 Ford F150 with NY plates approaching the corner of Brown Place and Monsignor Ryan Boulevard. As they got in line Andrew took note of the surrounding structures. He watched the movement of people while the drug orders were being processed. He could see that most of the people were carrying, and that there was security with rifles at several locations. As the pickup slowly moved in line, he found the central location that he believed where the drugs were stored. At one tenement window he saw a guy holding an AK-47. They came to the head of the line and stopped. Andrew said,

"Give me three bags of H."

"That's $300 bucks."

He handed over the money and moved forward where they were given the heroin. With a wave of his hand Martin pulled out on the Boulevard and headed West.

Andrew had seen what he needed to see, and his attack plan was being formulated.

FIFTEEN

1968
The Four-One Squad Room

Blackman looked at Feeney over his desk, "Sean, look at some of these ballistic comparisons that we just got from Forensics."

"Jesus, a lot of tie ins here with other cases. Two of the bullets that hit Conway were matched up to two other murders in the Bronx."

"Maybe we might get a lead if we investigate the victims, see if there is a common connection."

"Got nothing to lose, cause we haven't much else to go on. I'll take the first name, see where it leads."

"I'll take the second name and check him out."

The detectives each went their separate ways, and by the next day had the following information.

Blackman had checked out the victim Oscar Della Villa.

He was killed on February 15, 1966 on the corner of Laconia and Waring Avenues, a 1:23PM. Witnesses say he was standing at the corner, when a man in a leather jacket and sunglasses came up behind him and shot him twice in the head. The assailant calmly walked to a car, got in, and drove off. No one saw a license plate. Della Villa had a record, all narcotics distribution. His previous conviction resulted in 2 years in the NY State Prison at Comstock, NY from 1963 to 1966. He was part of a Dominican drug gang called the Arguelas. Only known relative, a sister, Mia Dominguez, 1834 Third Ave, Bronx, NY. Blackman would try and locate her.

Feeney had the second name, Max Torres. Torres was found dead from a single gunshot to the head, in front of 1794 East 172nd Street, Bronx, NY. No witnesses. He also had a narcotics record, but no arrests or convictions. He was a dealer with a drug gang called the SB88. A mother named Rita Gomez of 5411 Pelham Parkway, Bronx, NY was listed as next of kin.

Both detectives conferred, and could see that narcotics distribution were the same in both murders. Blackman decided to call Pete Velasquez of Narcotics, maybe he may be able to provide more info.

"Hello Sarge, this is Blackman from the Four-One Squad."

"Yes, hey we haven't heard anything on the street regarding your case, will keep on it."

"Good, but that is not why I am calling for."

"What do you need?"

"Ever hear of the Arguelas and the SB88's?"

"Sure, they were once big distributors, with big territories, but they disappeared, like in a magic act. They never appeared again on the streets, they were pushed out by an even bigger gang from the Dominican Republic."

"What was the name of this gang?"

"The Toros, they work out of Brown Place and Monsignor Ryan, been there for a long time. Well organized and disciplined."

'Again Sarge, thanks for the info."

CHAPTER SIXTEEN

1968
Brown Place, the Bronx

THREE NON-DESCRIPT CARS waited in line to place their orders. Inside each car were two persons, heavily armored and armed. Across the rooftops two separately armed bands of men were entering their objectives from the top. Arrival on the fourth floor of the buildings, one of the invaders crept slowly up to an open door. Peering round the corner, he could see the rifleman sitting near the window. His back was turned and he was smoking. Never hearing the assassins approach, he felt the sharpness of the blade slide across his throat. Taking his position, the assassin picked up the rifle and stared out the window. At the building across the street, another new rifleman appeared at the window. The rest of the band continued

downward till they reached street level. There were
two other members just inside the hallway armed
with Uzi submachine pistols. In a fusillade of carefully
timed suppressed shots all three were dead. Again
the lookout in the doorway was replaced. One of the
building invaders clicked twice on his walkie-talkie.
The clicks were heard in the car. Andrew Conway told
the driver to beep his horn once. This was the signal
for thirty seconds left. The cars pulled up closer, as
a another customer was serviced. At the 29th second
the horn beeped, doors flew open and the assassins
stepped out firing at all observed targets. Within less
than a minute those on the street were dead. Those
that ran to the buildings for shelter were killed by
the rifleman, or fired upon when they entered the
ground hallways. It was expected that more Toro guns
would respond. Some came down the building stair-
ways from the above apartments, they were cut down
at the ground level entrance. In his top floor apartment Jaime Ordonez knew he had to flee for his life.
With his girlfriend and bodyguard they made for the
roof, but Andrew Conway had planned for this exit.
A sniper on a higher building above their roof exit
was waiting. Jaime took a single bullet to the head,
and plunged over the side to the sidewalk below. The
bodyguard lasted a few seconds longer guiding the
female to a back fire escape. He got hit in the back

and went down. The screaming female made it down to the fire escape to the street. Two figures awaited her. Both masked and dressed in camouflage clothing bearing weapons, stopped her in her tracks.

"We are not going to kill you. Take this message back to your island."

He gave her a simple business card with the word, "Seaford Inc.". Andrew Conway told her to go, and she ran off down the avenue. The oval and anchor had gained their revenge.

CHAPTER SEVENTEEN

1968
Four-One Precinct, thirty minutes later.

T HE RADIOS AND phones were blaring, massacre in the South Bronx. All hell was breaking loose. When Blackman and Feeney heard the address they stopped in their tracks. Both looked at each other with surprised expressions. They knew that whatever link they had uncovered was gone. This case had taken a new direction, and the murder of Vincent Conway Jr. would never be solved. They now had a new case to piece together, and people to interview. Arriving at the scene, they were both startled at the number of dead bodies. Soon more reports were pouring in from more bodies in the adjacent buildings.

It took three days to identify the body of Jaime Ordonez.

The killing shot was identified, and they found the bodyguard still up on the roof. About a week later, an older lady remembered seeing a female in a red skirt going down the fire escape. She could not see if she ever made it to the street. The investigation went on for months with no suspects or reasons for the massacre. As far as the city power brokers were concerned, a public menace had been taken care of, time to forget about it and move on. It became official when Lt. Washington called both Feeney and Blackman into his office.

"What do you have on the Brown Place investigation?"

"Nothing, but we still have a few leads to check out." replied Blackman.

"Well as of right now both of you are stop your investigation, and this will be filed as a cold case"

Feeney,

"Hey LT, who ordered this bullshit We can get these perps."

"Listen you two, the brass has made the decision, the city administration is ecstatic about losing a whole drug gang, they want it buried and forgotten, we will do as ordered. Now get to your other cases and out of my office."

Years went by very little surfaced, and the investigation went from cold to frozen, but never forgotten by the two detective partners.

EIGHTEEN

1985
Somers Point, NJ

Morris "RED" BLACKMAN loved his boat. It was a Boston Whaler 345 Conquest with triple Mercury outboards, the family and grandkids loved it, he was able to get to the prime fishing grounds, and now life was good. Retired as a NYPD Captain of Detectives in 1983, he moved the family to the Jersey Shore. With a boat slip in Somers Point and a beautiful home in Tuckahoe, NJ he was enjoying retirement. However something was lacking, he needed to work, even if was minimal, so he got in touch with a corporate headhunter. His search ended when he was to be interviewed by a small pharmaceutical company in Dorothy, NJ. They were looking for a Corporate Security Manager, and his credentials were above and beyond the job criteria. He told them to make him an offer. He knew it would be somewhat below what he could get in NYC or Philadelphia, but he would sacrifice the money to be close to his family. They agreed on a salary, and Blackman was hired as the new Security Manager in charge of a 250 person manufacturing plant for Attentive Pharmaceuticals. He was back to work and was very happy. He was well liked and respected by management and the employees because he took an interest in their safety and security. In his office he made his monthly call to his old partner Feeney.

"Hello is this the drunken Irishman?"

"Bagels, how are you?"

"Great, I apprehended a burglar, it was a squirrel who got into cafeteria storage."

"Did he get the death penalty?"

"No we like animals here. How's the squad Lt. Feeney?

"Busy as a bitch, two murders last night, all narcotics related. Miss this shit?"

"Not even close. It is so quiet here; the most strenuous I do is walk a terminated employee out of the plant. Hey, Beerman, when are you set to retire? Come down here, we'll have fun again?"

"As you say Red, not even close. Three more years,

then the girlfriend and I are ready for Florida. I'll make sure we will have a room for you and the wife."

"Ok buddy, keep in touch, stay safe."

"Will do Red."

NINETEEN

1985
New Seaford Incorporated Headquarters
1773 Fire Road, Northfield, NJ

I N THE 8ᵀᴴ floor Executive suite of the CEO, Andrew Conway gazed at the skyline of Atlantic City. As the head of the Conway Empire, Andrew had expanded the business making it profitable and legitimate. On paper, and to the rest of world Seaford Inc., was a major supplier to the Gaming Industry. Everything a Casino needed they supplied from bed linens to Roulette wheels. Andrew had even gotten the company on the NASDAQ exchange. Most of the employed relatives were college educated and degreed with specialties in tax law, labor law, and acquisitions. The Conway family tree had branched out to the highest of the American social order. Andrew's son Mark, was the present United States Senator for New Jersey. Martin Conway's oldest daughter was married to a United States Appellate Judge in Pennsylvania. The world may have changed the company, but the company had not. Despite its current wealth, the basis for its power was still smuggling which accounted for over 55% of its wealth, and Andrew was committed to keep it that way.

Under the cover of various businesses like waste management, maritime services, food purveyors, and barrel manufacturing the old ways continued. Both coasts of America made money for the corporation, each entity overseen by a new family member with the oval globe and anchor tattoo.

The trouble started in Delaware on a Wednesday morning in June. Ralph Blaine head of DelMarVa Ship and Tool, located in Holt's Landing, Delaware was in his office. He was awaiting the arrival of his two sons. The boys Patrick and Tim had met an offshore Panamanian freighter at 3AM and loaded some two tons of cocaine onto their 42 foot Huntress. With a speed over water at 80 mph plus, the boat would reach the DelMarVa dock within the hour. With Patrick at the controls, the noise of the engines shut out the noise of the approaching helicopter from the boat's rear. As the chopper got closer, a sharpshooter inside aligned his sights and fired once striking Patrick in the head.

The boat slowed to a halt, Tim was sleeping below when he noticed they had stopped, he climbed up the ladder to the deck. He found his brother lying in his own blood, and two men with pistols pointed directly at him. One of the men spoke,

"What's your name?"

"Tim Blaine."

It was answered with a shot to his stomach. He went down hard.

In a Spanish accent the man who shot him got down close to him and said.

"You've been gut shot, you will die, but in dying you will take a message to your family. They will wonder who killed you, and they will never know for we are the avengers."

Tim was tied to a harness and raised into the helicopter. The shooter followed and the chopper headed in a northwest direction. Patricks' body was thrown overboard, and the remaining man took control of the boat and headed south. Ralph became concerned at 4AM when the boat hadn't arrived within the hour. He would wait another hour before making the required calls. It was still dark on the Delaware mainland. The helicopter was heading up to the Pine Barrens to drop its load when a violent wind gust blew it to the left then up. Tim, near death, was not secured and he rolled out the door and fell some 600 feet down towards the ground. The fall finished him off, and the helicopter was not going to search for the body, so it turned and flew south. Ralph Blaine did not call the Coast Guard, he called his first cousin Andrew Conway.

 # CHAPTER TWENTY

1985
Attentive Pharmaceuticals Manufacturing Plant
Dorothy, NJ

R ED BLACKMAN WOKE up everyday at 6 AM, took a shower, then got into car and headed to his favorite coffee shop in Tuckahoe, *Captain Mullicas*. Red ordered the 16 oz. coffee and a Taylor pork roll and egg on a seeded Kaiser roll. He always sat at the counter and watched the morning Philadelphia news on the TV above the coffee machine. Nothing out of the ordinary was happening that morning, but that would change once his beeper was activated. He looked at the number and saw it was the plant. Getting off his stool, he walked over to the pay phone and called in. The phone was answered,

"Good Morning, Attentive Pharma Security, Officer Hippel speaking."

"Bobby, this is Red, what do you need?

"Red, we have a problem. The mobile patrol found a dead body inside the fence line on the North side. The guy is dead. We haven't touched anything, what do you want me to do?"

"I'm about 10 minutes out, leaving now. Call the State Police, then notify the shift supervisor inside, and advise him I am on my way in and for him to no-tify the plant manager. I want the North road tapped off, no traffic."

"Ok, Red, will do."

As Blackman left the coffee shop, he started his car and headed up Route 557. He began to think about the North side of the plant, it was an 8 foot high chain link fence topped with 3 strands of barbed wire, the barbed wire added another 2 feet. Behind that fence was nothing but trees and brush, almost 39 miles of natural woods and streams that were part of the Pine Barrens of New Jersey. How did a body get inside to the plant property? He pulled up to main gate, Bobby Hippel rushed out and Red rolled down his window.

"Boss, the road is tapped off. I called the State Police right after I spoke to you, and they were send-ing a Trooper, he has not arrived yet. I also notified

Henry Consalves inside, and he was alerting the Plant Manager."

"Good Bobby, I'm going back to the fence line, get me on the radio, when the trooper arrives."

Hippel nodded and Blackman drove down the East Road. The plant occupied a large parcel of land which measured a perfect square off of Atlantic County route 557. The east road was a half-mile long, then he turned right onto the north road. He got out and moved aside the tape, then drove about a quarter mile to where his mobile patrol vehicle was parked with lights flashing.

Getting out of his car he was met by George Parker, a longtime Security Officer at the plant.

"Morning Red, this is something. Nearly scared the hell out of me. I found him at 6:20AM. There was nothing here on the 4:45 to 5:30AM patrol."

Parker's hand held lantern illuminated the scene. Blackman could see that the fence had been damaged, and the body was very bloody around the torso. He would wait for the State Trooper, for this may have occurred on plant property, but it was a police matter, and he was no longer a cop.

"George, keep the tape up on the Northwest corner, and you pull your vehicle to the Northeast corner and block access, only let the trooper in. I be here in my car"

Parker nodded and left, Blackman went to sit in

his car. He was glad he had wrapped up the sandwich and capped the coffee. It was almost an hour since the call, that the Trooper finally arrived. Hippel called Blackman on the radio, and Parker allowed him access to the North Road. As the Trooper got out, Blackman exited his car and went over to introduce himself.

""Good morning Trooper, I'm Red Blackman head of Security. One of my officers discovered this at 6:20 AM while on patrol. We haven't touched anything."

The Trooper, who appeared to be about 25 years old just looked at Blackman, never said his name, and started walking in the direction of the body. Blackman knew that the proper approach was to determine an outer ring and examine in a walking circle, each time getting closer to the body. You might find some evidence away from the body, and this could help the investigation, but this guy went charging in. As he got to the body he looked down, and started turning green. Instead of moving away, he vomited right over the corpse. Blackman was beside himself, but held back. The Trooper started walking back to his car, passing Blackman, then sat in his cruiser on the front passenger side. He sat and did not move for the next ten minutes. Blackman came over and asked him if he was all right.

"I'll be ok, never saw a body like that."

"Well in this line of work, you may see more."

"I'm going to call for a Detective-Trooper, they have more experience for this."

"Didn't they train you in basic crime scene investigation and area technique?"

"Yes, they did, but that body really made me sick."

"What is your name Trooper? You never introduced yourself."

"Trooper Willis Harvey. You know I don't need questions from some private security jerk!"

"Your right Trooper Harvey, I have no right to question your credentials. I'll just sit in my car and wait for the Detective."

Blackman returned to his car and radioed the front gate "Bobby, this Trooper is calling in a State Police Detective, make sure you let me know that he is coming back."

"Ok, Red."

Blackman had learned long ago never to talk to ignorant cops. They were only doing the job with the least amount of effort, and counted the days toward retirement. You could not count on them in a fight or for backup. It was part of the profession that unfortunately existed. It was about an hour later that the State Police Detective arrived. He got out of his unmarked car and went over to the Trooper still sitting in the car. The conversation was through the rolled down window. It ended, and the Detective came over to Blackman's car.

"Good morning, I'm Sgt. Dan Stansfield. I understand you're the head of Security?

"Yes, I'm Red Blackman. As I first told the trooper one of my officers on patrol found the body at 6:20AM.

That same officer was previously past this point on the 4:45 to 5:30 AM patrol and there was nothing here."

"Is that officer still here?"

"Yes, he's the one you passed when you turned the corner."

"Any chance you can hold him over, I'll need his statement."

"Sure, no problem."

"To your knowledge has anybody touched the body?"

Blackman thought to himself, and then gave the best answer.

"Better talk to Trooper Willis Harvey over there."

Stansfield knew something had happened, and went over to Harvey. Blackman could see the argument that ensued, then Stansfield walked way to his car and starting talking into his radio. For the next hour Stansfield sat in his car, and Trooper Harvey in his.

Hippel called on the radio for Blackman.

"Red, I got another Trooper here."

"Let him thru, Bobby."

Within two minutes a State Police car pulls up and a uniformed Lieutenant exits. He goes over to Stansfield's car and talks, and then goes over to Harvey's car. He tells Harvey to get out of his car and calls him to attention. Blackman now realized this is the Station Commander. Harvey is ramrod straight at attention and sweating. In the next five minutes the Officer literally skinned Trooper Harvey alive. Harvey 's face was beet red, when the Lt. yelled,

"You're dismissed Trooper, return to Barracks now and put yourself on report!. Now get the hell out of my sight!"

Harvey did an about face and got into his car and took off. The Lt. and Stansfield then approached Blackman.

The Lt. spoke first,

"My name is Lt. Tom Armistead, station commander Troop "A", our apologies Mr. Blackman to you and your company, we usually take great pride in our organization, and assure you that Trooper will never set foot on this property or any other property within my command. I assure you that Detective Stansfield has my confidence, and will continue with this investigation."

Blackman just nodded, and watched as the Lt. got in his car and drove off.

Stansfield,

"Mr. Blackman, do you have a business card?"

"Yes, I do." Reaching for his wallet he opened it and Stansfield saw Blackman's NYPD shield.

"You're ex-NYPD?"

He handed Stansfield his business card, and said,

"Retired after 32 years."

"I've been doing this for 24 years, and will probably pull the pin in 6 more years. Where did you work in the city?"

"South Bronx, it was another world."

"Well let me get an Medical Examiner in here. Then I'll be out of here, and you people can get back the use of this road."

Blackman shook Stansfield's hand and told him he would be in his office if needed.

Back in his office he called the plant manager to let him know the State Police were in charge and that he would keep in touch with them on any updates. Throughout the morning and into the afternoon the state detective had the county Medical Examiner in to do his initial scene findings and to remove the body. A Forensics team was brought in he had left the scene still tapped. On his way out Stansfield called Blackman from the gate,

"Mr. Blackman, we have everything we need, and many thanks for your time.

"No problem, and good luck with this case."

 CHAPTER TWENTY-ONE

1985
New Seaford Incorporated, Northfield, NJ

THE CALL FROM Ralph Blaine was most distressing, for approximately $4 million of cocaine was gone. Not knowing if the boat sank, or was it hi-jacked? Andrew Conway was worried. Andrew called a paid informant in the Coast Guard Station in Cape May to see if any mayday signals were received, the answer was negative. He then made an overseas call to the owner of the Panamanian ship from which the cocaine was offloaded. He was told the transfer was completed in the early morning hours and the cigarette boat left fully loaded. He wondered who would raise a hand against Seaford? All knew their reputation for revenge. However, he hadn't counted on a long-standing hate and need for revenge that emanated from the city of Banao, Dominican Republic.

CHAPTER TWENTY-TWO

1985
Banao, Dominican Republic

WHEN HIS BROTHERS had died in NY, Pedro Ordonez was a college student in Madrid Spain. He was considered the one who would be a doctor or maybe a judge, but his education was abruptly ended, and he was called home. With an orderly and business like mind, he transformed the family drug business from a gang of street sellers to a world-wide distribution network. When Jaime's girlfriend Eva Corona had brought the message from Seaford, Pedro knew he must not act in haste. Vengeance would be put on the back burner, and simmer slowly, for he had to re-build the Banao family business from the ground up making it stronger with more viable markets. It may take years, but the goal was to achieve wealth and power.

Jaime and Ramon would be avenged in due time, and the dogs at Seaford would be obliterated. Today Pedro ran a network of distribution that reached into Europe and Asia. He had made deals with groups that others shunned, such as the Muslim Brotherhood. From operational bases in the North of Africa thru the Middle East, he received the product. In turn he smuggled it into the United States thru Mexico and Florida. As he grew his network, the money came in like a flood. Money provided the means to corrupt high officials, and to get the needed intelligence. Pedro studied Seaford and its many ventures. As the years went by he waited for the right time to make his move. In the meantime, he would be the mosquito that quickly bit them here and there, never causing a major stoppage, just an annoyance. Through his sources, he learned of the cocaine transfer at sea. It was just a matter of properly coordinating the cigarette boat's interception that would definitely annoy the mighty Andrew Conway.

CHAPTER TWENTY-THREE

1985
Atlantic County Medical Examiner Office
Atlantic City, NJ

STATE POLICE DETECTIVE Stansfield watched as the pathologist complete the autopsy. He waited for the doctor to dispose of his gown and mask, and wash up.

"What can you tell me Doc?"

"The deceased was alive until he fell into that fence."

"I thought he died of a gunshot to the gut."

"He had a 9mm bullet in his liver, but there was extreme shock to the body as if he had fallen from a great height. The top of the fence went into his neck and punctured the main artery that was the cause of death. The force of the fall shattered bones and collapsed his spine. He had all the signs of one who jumped from a high building."

"You're saying he fell from a very high height."

"Yes, This height was well over some 500 feet."

"Anything else?"

"Well he had traces of cocaine in his system. We took his fingerprints, and some photos of a tattoo on the inside of his right arm. There was evidence of a rope wrapped around his chest and under his armpits, as if he had been raised. When the prints come back, I'll send you the final package."

"Thanks, Doc."

Stansfield left the ME Office for his office at the Bass River station. Grabbing a cup of hot coffee he sat down and began to study parts of the report from Forensics.

- "uncovered blood on fence along with some body matter which will be determined."
- "ground beneath the body showed a three and half inch depression in the ground. See photo."

He said to himself, the Doc was right, he did fall from a height. Well now I have to wait for an identification.

As he sipped his coffee, he needed to do one more thing. He pulled out Blackman's business card. Though not related to the case, he needed to know who was Morris Blackman? Stansfield had a NYPD connection, His brother-in-law Pete Whitlock was a Detective in Manhattan, he would give him a call.

"Hello Nine-Squad, Detective Mickelson."

"I'd like to speak to Detective Whitlock."

"Please hold, I'll connect you."

He waited about 2 minutes, then he heard his brother-in-law.

"Hello, this is Detective Whitlock."

"Hey Pete, staying out of trouble I hope?

"Danny boy, how are you? You know your sister was talking about you the other night, she wants to get everybody together for Thanksgiving."

"My luck, I'll probably be working that night. How are the kids?

"Great, Michelle lost her top teeth, and little Pete Jr. just took his first steps. They are all fine, what are you up to?

"Working on a case down here, homicide in the middle of nowhere. It appears the body fell from the sky, maybe the Jersey Devil dropped him as he flew by."

"Danny you know that Jersey Devil scares the shit out of me."

"You big baby, it is a bunch of legends that someone made up. Anyway, I called you if you knew of a retired NYPD cop, who runs security at the place where we found the body? He appears to be a nice guy, had his badge in his wallet, name is Morris Blackman, goes by the nickname Red. Have you ever heard of him?"

Pete was silent for a few seconds, then asked,

"Did you say Morris "Red" Blackman?"

"Yes."

"He's a legend. Retired as Captain of Detectives, Bronx South. He and his partner were known as Bagels and Beer, the most successful case closing team in the history of the department. I heard him speak at a Detective training session about 6 years ago, he was terrific, man knows his craft. All I can say Danny is that if you want to solve this case, make him your partner."

Stansfield said,

"Thanks Pete for the information, give Jenny my love and kiss the kids."

"Good luck Danny."

CHAPTER TWENTY-FOUR

1985
33 English Creek Road, Tuckahoe, NJ

THE WEEKEND WAS upon him and he was looking forward to taking the boat out for some time on the ocean, but the duty of a homeowner called. His home sat on a four acre lot, and most of it was the front lawn. Red Blackman went to his shed and started up his lawn tractor, he really liked sitting on the tractor and mowing his lawn, it relaxed him. He and his wife loved the place for its privacy and great shore location. With a set of Bose headphones he plugged into his Sony transistor radio and had the Yankees versus Red Sox game. It would take him about two hours to complete his mowing, and then he would hit the fridge for a bottle of Corona, with a cut of lime and he was in heaven. For some reason, he thought about the body found at the plant. That body had fallen from the sky. He knew by the grass impression, and there was no reported air crashes in the area. The body was that of a boater, the shoes were the giveaway, and he seen a carabineer hanging from his belt. The carabineer was used a safety clip to keep one on the bridge during a rocky voyage. He suddenly stopped, and told himself that it was no concern of his, he was retired, others would have that task of how and why. The Yankees were ahead by one run, going into the bottom of the ninth, Red Sox were coming to bat. Phil Niekro had pitched eight innings, so they brought in closer Dave Righetti to stop the Sox. Dewey Evans flied out to left field, Jim Rice singled, and Wade Boggs hit a long center field shot caught for the second out, but Rice advanced to second. Mike Greenwell fouled off the ball 5 times, Blackman was sweating. Then Righetti reared back and threw a 96 mph fastball, Greenwell swung and missed. The Yankees won, and Blackman let out a cheer that no one heard, because his closest neighbor was a half mile down the road. As he sat there he kept thinking about the body, as if he was back on the case.

TWENTY-FIVE

1985
NJ State Police, Bass River Station.

D AN STANSFIELD GOT the packet from the Medical Examiner. The fingerprints identified the body as Timothy Blaine of 537 Cove Road, Bethany Beach, Delaware. Born 3/6/1960 in Milford, Delaware. With this Stansfield typed in a FBI Criminal History Request, and waited about two hours. What came back was an arrest and conviction for receiving stolen property in Rehoboth Beach in 1979 Mr. Blaine served 6 months in the county lockup and paid a $500 fine. There were no other convictions. He called the Delaware State Police for them to find the next of kin and for the family to contact him in NJ. This case was a puzzle that needed to be pieced together, and all he could do now was slowly go thru the paces and maybe a lead may surface.

CHAPTER TWENTY-SIX

1985
15 Surf Road, Holt's Landing, Delaware

T HE ARRIVAL OF the Delaware State Police car at
Ralph Blaine's home was not expected. His wife
took the news hard, and fainted. Ralph had an idea
of something wrong had happened, but kept his emo-
tions covered.

He asked the Trooper, if they knew anything about
his other son. The Trooper only had the information on
Timothy, it would be best to contact this NJ Detective
Stansfield. His first call was to Andrew Conway.

"Andrew, Tim was found dead in New Jersey, nobody knows nothing about Patrick. They told me to
call a State Police Detective in Jersey, probably to identify the body."

"That would be their next step in their investigation.

Look, Ralph I am so sorry about this, but this our business, and with it sometimes come the reality of death. Call this cop, go up to Jersey and find out what you can about where he was found. I got the word out on Patrick, but so far nothing. We are looking for the boat up and down the eastern seaboard. Be strong cousin."

After he finished with Ralph, Andrew got another call from his cousin Richie Conway. Richie was Andrew's muscle.

"Andrew, we found the boat. It was tied to a slip at a marina in Ocean City, Maryland, and it was empty."

"Anybody see who brought it in?"

"No, they found it when they opened at 7 AM. The Ocean City Police impounded it. I will call Ralph to report the boat was taken,"

"Alright Ritchie put the word out we've been ripped off and will pay for information."

"Okay, Andrew, will do"

Andrew sat back and began to rack his mind as who may have pulled off this heist, and could not think of anyone.

CHAPTER TWENTY-SEVEN

1985
Atlantic County Medical Examiners Office

STANSFIELD MET RALPH Blaine and took him to the morgue. He made a positive identification of the body as his son Timothy Blaine. As they left the morgue, Blaine asked,

"Where did you find my son's body?"

"Behind a factory in Dorothy, NJ."

"Your saying he may been killed at the factory?"

"No, Mr. Blaine, the body was found in the rear of the property by a patrolling security officer. It appeared the body had fallen from a height, like from an airplane. Your son was shot in the stomach, but was still alive when he fell, he hit a fence ands that is what caused his death. Do you know anyone who had it in for your son?"

"No, Tim was well liked."

"The autopsy revealed he had cocaine in his system. Did he use cocaine?

"No, Tim only drank beer and hardly was ever drunk."

"Did your son have a job?"

"Yes, he worked for my company DelMarVa Ship and Tool Co. We're out of Holt's Landing and do Marine repairs. He was a good welder and fabricator."

"Where did he live?"

"Bethany Beach, he had a condo."

"Any girl friends or wives?"

"No he lived alone, he had girls friends, but never married."

'Do you have any other children who may have known where Tim may have been?

"Patrick his brother, but we have not seen Patrick for about 2 years, he left the business some time ago."

"Well, I appreciate your time Mr. Blaine, again my condolences. The ME will be right in to discuss your arrangements for the transportation of the body."

"Thank you, Detective."

CHAPTER TWENTY-EIGHT

1985
New Seaford Incorporated

T HE BUSINESS HAD to go on, despite this costly in-
terruption. Andrew Conway checked his appoint-
ment book and saw there was a very important meeting coming up. As stockholder's wanted to know what
their company was doing, so did the family Clan.
It was Andrew's responsibility to report on the state
of affairs of Seaford Incorporated. Held at an estate
owned by the company, it was on the original land
once owned by William Conway in Waretown. A
huge outdoor tent would act as the main meeting place
followed by a gala party that all enjoyed. Andrew had
to work on the annual speech reporting on the successful ventures that were making money. Every Conway,
Blaine and Thompson would be in attendance not just

to hear a speech, but also to collect his or her share. Decreed by the legendary Roger Conway in 1910.

"The Clan shall meet once every year to hear what the business has made, and each of us will be paid their fair share."

It was Andrew's duty as leader of the Clan to open the books and coffers. He knew the family very well and he would have to be prepared for questioning from the elites. It was this group that tried to ignore the criminal side of the business, but would be very vocal regarding any operation that failed, such as the lost cocaine transfer. The remainder of the clan was made up of the blue collar relatives, those that worked for and supported all the aspects of the family business and were very loyal to Andrew. It was these people that were the power behind Andrew. Andrew's own father Reggie had told him,

"Son, my own brother is a United States Congressman and if I needed him to cover my back, he would back away because in his mind a man of his stature does not get dirty his hands, but my second cousin who fixes my trucks would stop a bullet for me. As leader of the Clan, you must use the family members as you see fit. The Congressman will make calls for you and doors will open, the second cousin will work his ass off to make sure you have trucks, and carry a gun when you hit an enemy."

Andrew called in his sister Abigail. She was the Chief Financial Office of Seaford. A Certified Public Accountant and graduate of the Wharton School of Business, she was Andrew's baby sister by some 10 years, and very loyal to the family. It was said Reggie would have made her the head of the Clan due to her intelligence, but a female was forbidden.

"Abby, I'm preparing my speech for the Clan annual meeting. What will be the share per family member for this year?"

"There are 30 eligible shares this year, that is an increase of two over last year. We netted $15 million for the shareowners, which translates to $500 thousand for each eligible member."

"Good, that's about $20 thousand more than last year."

"As always it be paid out in cash, right after your speech."

"Our long range investment portfolio?"

"Cousin Mark Conway and his Wall Street firm have put us in a good position with a return on investment over 12% per annum. Last look at that account was over $780 million. Andrew, we are in very good financial shape."

"And our present Seaford Incorporated ventures and operations?"

"Seaford is worth some $6.5 billion. HTB

acquisition will be finalized next month, and with our takeover you can add another $2 billion."

HTB was a South Korean shipbuilding company that had in the past built some 6 ships for Seaford. Abigail, one year ago approached the owner and inquired if they wanted to sell their company. He agreed and for the past year the acquisition was being finalized.

Andrew,

"Abby, have you been working with the boat designers on the specific ship we require?"

"Those designs were recently approved by our sea architects, and our hidden holds will carry some 500 tons of contraband."

"Very good baby sister. Now to something more important, when is Dr. Norman going to put a

ring on your finger?"

"He said once he becomes Head of Surgery, we get hitched."

"Good and I will walk you down the aisle."

"Wouldn't want it any other way, big brother."

CHAPTER TWENTY-NINE

1985
Bass River Station, NJSP

I T HAD BEEN six weeks since the discovery of Timothy Blaine's body at Attentive Pharmaceuticals and so far no new leads. Stansfield literally had nothing new. All he had was an identified male body with little else. He had run another check on Blaine, and nothing other than his known past arrest and conviction. His employment was with his father's company was confirmed. He had reported a gross income of sixty-two thousand dollars on his federal taxes listing his occupation as a welder. Stansfield had re-contacted the Delaware State Police and obtained a search warrant for the victim's condo in Bethany Beach, the search yielded nothing. With the Christmas holidays approaching his investigation remained dormant, but outside forces were to show some new results. The ocean waters around Delaware and New Jersey are in constant motion due to the influence of the Gulf Stream or the occasional hurricane coming up from the south. A fisherman at Sandy Hook National Park was sitting on a dark beach in his beach chair, with his Coleman lantern lit, and about 300 foot of line awaiting a striper hit. He had been sitting there for the last 5 hours, and decided to get up and walk around. Placing his rod in a rod holder he walked maybe twenty feet away, when he tripped over something. He went back to retrieve his lantern and came back to discover a weed covered body. He ran to his car and drove to a 24 hour WAWA market. He told them what he found, and for them to call the Police. The local police showed up at the market, and followed the fisherman back to the beach. Returning to the spot they verified it was a body, and put out the call. The next morning the news had hit the television news and the newspapers. It would take a few days to identify the body. Within a week, the body was identified as Patrick Blaine of Milford, Delaware. To the average citizen this was a tragedy, especially before the holiday season, but to Detective Stansfield this was a good lead. Stansfield made the trip up to Monmouth County and met with the investigating officers. They were calling it a homicide, since the victim was shot in the head. Forensics had identified the bullet as .308

caliber rifle bullet. When Stansfield told them of his investigation, the local detectives turned over all the evidence they had to him, Their Chief knew an investigation by his department was not in their department's interest, so he deferred to the State authority. Stansfield now had the homicide investigation of two brothers, and it was here that he realized he needed the help of Red Blackman.

CHAPTER THIRTY

1986
Banao, Dominican Republic

PEDRO ORDONEZ WAS busy with his new venture, Chrystal Meth. Using his bases in North Africa he had brought in the chemists and "cookers" to produce a product he could distribute in Europe. France, Italy and Spain would be the trial areas. If it was a success, he estimated a market value of over $350 million. It was also time for another attack against Seaford. His people in New York had viewed the property at 156 Beard Street, Brooklyn as a major warehouse, and recommended it be destroyed. It was planned for St. Valentines Eve. A team of five would enter and take out whatever security was there. Each one carried a 5 gallon container of gasoline. A single security guard was at the truck gate, he was subdued and tied up.

Entering the warehouse, they all sped off in different directions. Finding areas that contained weapons and ammunition, cocaine and marijuana, liquor, and computer equipment they started an inferno. Leaving as swiftly as they arrived, the fire was at full intensity when the first fire units arrived. It went to 8 alarms and continued burning into the next day. Andrew was furious, he vowed if he found them, he would personally kill them. The loss of 156 Beard Street put a dent into the Seaford operation, not fatal, but expensive to replace. More money was put out on the street to find the firebugs, but the Toros had become ghosts.

CHAPTER THIRTY-ONE

1986
Attentive Pharmaceuticals, Dorothy, NJ

Eating his morning pork roll and egg sandwich at *Captain Mullicas*, he started to sip his coffee, when the Philadelphia news program showed a fire in Brooklyn. The on site reporter was telling how difficult the fire was for the firefighters. It had gone to 8 alarms and that they had just brought it under control. As the reporter signed off Red heard him say,

"This entire building has been destroyed. From the Seaford International fire on Beard Street in the Red Hook section of Brooklyn, this is Alejandro Rios for WABC channel 10."

He perked up, and he remembered that day when he and his partner found the spot where a traffic ticket was issued. Coincidence, maybe, that case still bothered him after all these years. There was never enough connecting evidence that would have gotten them the right leads. He finished his sandwich, wished everybody a good day, and left for the plant. As he entered the front gate, Bobby Hippel came out to tell him he had a visitor waiting for him in the lobby. He parked his car and entered the front entrance to find someone who looked familiar. It took him a few seconds to remember the face, he said.

"Detective Stansfield right?"

Stansfield was amazed he remembered him.

"Your good, Mr. Blackman."

"Call me Red. What can I do for you?

"I'd like to run something by you, if you have the time."

"Sure, let's get some coffee and sit in my office, it's more private."

They picked up two coffees at the cafeteria, then went to Blackman's office. Stansfield started,

"Red, the body that was found here, has been a tough investigation. For all intent and purposes someone shot him, and in falling the fence got him, and that was the cause of death. Why and where he fell from is still a mystery. His autopsy showed he had cocaine in his system, but his father never knew he was a user. He had a record, served time in a county lockup, and again he never got in trouble again. Worked as a welder for the family business, and lived a bachelor's life. I have yet to uncover anything that would give me a lead."

Blackman thought to himself that he was thinking the same thing this morning regarding an old unsolved case.

"This case has gone nowhere for the past 7 months, when all of a sudden a body washes up on a Sandy Hook beach with a head shot from a .308 rifle. The victim was the brother of the victim you found here. When I interviewed the father, he said he hadn't seen this son for over 2 years, yet he only lived about 30 miles away in the same county. I now have both murders to investigate, and I am getting the feeling there are no leads to be had. I thought maybe in your time you may had something similar, any ideas?

"Can I call you Dan?"

"Sure."

"Dan, it is very coincidental that this very morning I was watching the morning news and a location was being reported on for a case we never solved. Very similar to what you have, nothing evolving into a lead."

"Red, would you work with me on this one? I'll show you everything I have, and maybe you will see something I haven't."

Blackman thought for a moment, maybe it would be fun to get back in the saddle if for only this case, sure beats walking out terminated employees.

"I'll help, but you have to realize the fact that I work here, and I am obligated to Attentive. As long as I help you in my spare time, and not conflict with my duties here."

"I can work around that."

"An off-site place would be better. The best times for me are after work, so you find the place and I will be there."

"That's great. Let's meet tomorrow at the Bass River Station, around 6:30PM. Sound good?"

"Meet you then."

They shook hands, and a happy Stansfield left the office.

# THIRTY-TWO

1986
Port of Salem, NJ

A NDREW'S FATHER REGGIE in the early seventies had purchased the first ocean going ship for Seaford. Called the *Tiger Star*, she was a general cargo ship measuring 106 meters long and coming in at 2685 tons. Tiger Star was flagged in the Marshall Islands and plied all the world oceans carrying cargo both legal and illegal for Seaford. Andrew needed a test bed for his new design ship class, so the old Tiger Star was sent to a South Korean shipyard for some renovations. At a cost of some half a million dollars, Andrew's vision of a hidden hold was reality. Packed to the gills with Chinese lawn furniture and computers, the *Tiger Star* unloaded at Port Salem, NJ. U.S. Customs came aboard and watched the unloading. After some inspections the Customs officials gave here a clean bill of delivery. *Tiger Star's* captain, a Filipino named Arturo Bracos smiled as tugs guiding his ship back into Delaware Bay. He gave his navigator a course which would bring him to a deep-water inlet north of Tuckerton, NJ. Seaford had paid some $2.5 million to dredge a deep-water channel that would bring a ship a mile up an inlet to a shipyard repair facility owned by Seaford and managed by DelMarVa Ship and Repair. With the ship tied to the dock, the land crew went to work. Captain Bracos opened a hidden panel of buttons and sounds of movement came from the rear number five hold. Steel walls on track were raised and another hold was exposed. With a capacity of some 500 tons this was the "secret" hold that Andrew had envisioned and now was being incorporating in his new line of ships from South Korea. The cranes were lowered and soon some 1000 crates containing Fentanyl from China were unloaded and were divided amongst some five trucks that departed in different directions. A locked chest was delivered up from the hold to the DelMarVa office. The site manager Anthony Conway, Andrews son, opened the chest and removed 25 ingots of gold. Each ingot weighed 400 Troy ounces. He placed 23 in the office safe and sent 2 ingots to the *Tiger Star's* bridge where a grateful Captain Bracos received his cut. The experiment was successful, Andrew could now deliver legitimate goods, get unloaded and certified that his ship was empty. Using the inlet shipyard he would pull in for a repair and unload the hidden hold. The dredged channel inlet had already paid for itself, now Seaford would reap the rewards with its new class of cargo carriers.

 # THIRTY-THREE

1986
NJ State Police Station, Bass River, NJ

RED BLACKMAN ARRIVED at 6:30PM, asked for Detective Stansfield. A few minutes later Stansfield came out and escorted him to his office. The office was larger than most with a large table in the middle, on top were the two case folders. Standing, Stansfield went over the first case involving the death of Timothy Blaine. Blaine was shot in the stomach by a single 9mm bullet, threatening, but not fatal. A deep wound in his neck was the cause of death, severing a major artery. This was consistent with blood and material found on the fence. It was also determined that compression of the ground would have been a drop from the sky of some 500 feet.

Blackman,

"Dan, 500 feet up that is pretty high. So you're talking some type of aircraft. Was there any aircraft up at that hour? You know Pomona is a major air facility and has radar, have they been contacted?

"No, but will now make that request."

"Can I see the autopsy report?"

Blackman read it with interest. The part about the appearance the body had marks were rope related as if lifted up or raised. This would be consistent with being lifted up into a helicopter. Victim had cocaine in his system, tattoo inside right arm.

"Dan, you got any photos of this tattoo?

Stansfield pulled out a larger envelope and gave the photo to Blackman. Blackman eyes widened when he saw the oval and anchor. He silently put it down and stared at the photo.

Stansfield,

"You've seen this tat before?"

It took Blackman a few seconds to respond. The years ago suddenly came back.

"You said the other case was this victim's brother?

"Yes, Patrick Blaine."

"Did he have a tattoo?"

Stansfield, went to the folder and found the autopsy photo of the tattoo. He placed it on the table.

Blackman, put both photos together, they were exactly the same. The cold case in the Bronx was suddenly back on the burner.

"Dan, you retrieved two bullets from the victims?"

"Yes, a 9mm and a .308."

"Can, I make a long distance call?"

He dialed a number and waited.

"Is Lieutenant Feeney there?"

"Who's calling?"

"Red Blackman."

About a minute went by, when Feeney picked up.

"What's happening in the boonies?"

"Sean, listen up."

"Must be important, you only call me Sean when you got something good."

"Remember our cold case with the guy we took out of the water?"

"Yeah, that one still sticks in my craw."

"Well, I'm helping out a State Police Detective here on two homicides involving two brothers down here. One was gut shot with a 9mm, and the other head shot from a .308. Bodies turned up at two separate places. Autopsy photos showed both had an oval and anchor tattoo on their inner right arm."

Feeney.

"Holy Christ, the same as our guy."

"I am going to put Detective Dan Stansfield on.

He is going to send you the two bullets retrieved from the victims for comparison with the ballistics we got from Brown Place, give him your address and he'll FEDEX you the bullets. Sean, this may the break we never had."

"Ok Red,"

Blackman handed the phone to Stansfield, and waited while they talked. After about five minutes Stansfield hung up smiling.

"What so funny?"

"He said for me to hang on tight, the wild ride has begun."

CHAPTER THIRTY-FOUR

1986
Christmas Day
Ocean City, NJ

AT THE VERY end of Seaview Drive, the road came
to a cul-de-sac. A stone-wall and gate protected
some 30 acres of prime shore real estate. The quarter
mile driveway lead to a magnificent 10 bedroom brick
mansion. The mansion tonight was lit up for a holiday party, while some forty cars were being parked
by valets, the inside was very festive. The home and
property belonged to Andrew Conway and his wife
Cheryl. Family and friends had gathered for the annual dinner that was considered one of the highlights
of the year. Conway, Blaine and Thompson all min-
gled and talked. Elder Vincent Conway Sr. sat by a
roaring fire nursing his drink, looking about at all the

relatives. He saw the painting of the family's patriarch, William Conway, in his sea captain's uniform. He wondered what he would think of how far the family had come. Just then he heard a clinking of crystal, and heard a voice,

"May I have your attention? May I have your attention? We have an announcement."

It was Dr. Norman Phipps, Abby Conway's beau. Hand in hand the couple walked toward the fireplace then turned to the crowd. Phipps,

"It is with great joy to announce that Abby and I are engaged."

There was applause and cheer from the whole room, as they came forth with congratulations. Dr. Phipps had recently been named head of surgery at Jefferson Medical Center in Philadelphia. A superb four carat round diamond graced the hand of the female Conway, who was beaming with joy. As the crowd moved away from the fireplace, Andrew came over to Vincent.

"Cousin Vincent, may I wish you the spirits of the season and continued good health."

"Ah, Andrew, leader of the Clan. May the best of fortunes await you this Christmas season."

"Thank you. Has retirement been good to you?"

"As expected, lot of time to think, with little where to go.

I miss my Monica, we had so many plans"

"She was a lovely person, and she is missed."

"Well, what are you going to do now that Abby is betrothed and will move away?"

"She will still be part of the business. My father always said she was the smartest of the bunch. No Abby, will remain, she's to valuable to lose. With to-day's devices she can be in Tibet and still run her share of the business."

"Old Reggie, did have a knack of identifying talent, he was a unique individual."

"Yes, he was. He knew how to handle the Clan, and open new areas, some of which we are making a lot of money to date. Vincent, your son Mark, has provided us with a windfall of investments, you should be very proud of him."

"I am very proud of him, he is the son I tended to forget, while trying to guide another son. Mark, became the man I wanted Vinny Jr. to become."

The old man started to tear up, Andrew placed his hand on his shoulder.

"The family avenged Vinny Jr., it was no fault of yours.

My father always admired you above the others, he told me to seek your advice if I required it."

"How can I be of service Andrew?"

"Let's take our drinks to my study."

In the privacy and quietness of the study, the two men talked.

"Vincent, we soon will take ownership of six new ships, specifically built to our specifications. These new ships will increase our contraband volume by 200%, and we are already getting calls from some dubious sources that have offered us a lot of money."

"Tell me who contacted you?"

"The Islamist Revolutionaries want us to bring people into Europe. They are willing to pay us almost triple our price."

"And, have you returned an answer?"

"That is why I am asking you for advice."

"Andrew, walk away from this, it will hurt the Clan. Our whole business relies on getting the right doors open for us. To open those doors requires us to corrupt persons and businesses, and then put them in our pocket. We are an American enterprise, though not known, but still an enterprise that makes money. You do business with this ilk, we will be labeled as pariahs, and the full force of the Federal government will hit us like a bulldozer. For the sake of your grand-children and mine, walk away from this one."

Andrew thought about it for a few seconds then said,

"Thank you Vincent, these requests will politely be

denied, one must sometimes forget the lure of riches, and stay the course."

Vincent smiled, pointing to the portrait of William Conway.

"Even Old William agrees."

Andrew refilled his glass and they toasted the Christmas season.

THIRTY-FIVE

1987
N.J. State Police- Bass River

STANSFIELD AND BLACKMAN had a standing drywall board and the numerous drywall markers. There were three columns labeled as follows, Vincent Conway Jr., Timothy Blaine, and Patrick Blaine. Underneath each name was the month and year each died and location.

Blackman,

"Because of the tattoos, there is another factor that remains constant with these homicides, we just have to find it."

The phone rang and Stansfield picked it up.

"Sure, bring him to the conference room."

The door opened and a male entered.

Blackman,

"Sean Feeney meet Dan Stansfield."

They shook hands. Feeney came over to Blackman and hugged him. The two old partners smiled at each other, then sat at the table.

Feeney,

"I made copies of the case folder for Vincent Conway Jr. and the case folder for the Brown Place shoot-up. The ballistics on those bullets you retrieved have been identified. The 9mm that killed Timothy Blaine came from a pistol used in the shooting of Vincent Conway Jr.. The .308 rifle bullet that killed Patrick Blaine also came from a rifle used in the Conway shooting. They match the bullets removed at the Vincent Conway Jr. autopsy. So it seems we have mutual interests. Rabbi Blackman and Detective Stansfield besides the tattoos, what else do you have?"

Blackman,

"Nada, nothing, bupkus my Irish lad."

Feeney, looked at Stansfield and said,

"Now you can see what I had to put with all those years."

Stansfield smiled and said,

"Red briefed me on the Brown Place shoot-up, and that is when your investigation went south. Am I correct?"

"Yes."

"You had a lead the Toros may have murdered

Vincent Conway Jr. during a drug transaction, and before you could get to the Toros, they were all dead. Did you ever have any leads on who killed them?"

Feeney,

"We never even got a smell of anything. No pressure from the department because the city just lost an entire drug gang, and was elated. Red and I kept at it, but it died a slow death and went cold."

Blackman,

"Our narcotics sources also hit the wall. We all came to the same conclusion, and that was the shoot-up had all the aspects of a military operation. Unseen entry over the roof and down into the buildings. Posing as buyers, came out firing, it was well planned. Someone had military experience, and a good crew."

Stansfield,

"Do both of you believe this was in retaliation for Conway's murder?"

Both Blackman and Feeney nodded yes.

"Who was Vincent Conway Jr.? I know you found his apartment was cleaned before you got there, but again why was this guy so important that some group had to hit and wipe out a whole gang?"

Feeney,

"I wish I had the answer, but we somehow have your two vics with the same tattoo, and the same bullets from the guns used at Brown Place."

Blackman,

"The tattoos need to be researched, someone designed it, and someone put it to ink. I believe this particular tat may have originated down here or in Delaware."

Feeney,

"And how the hell did you come up with that one?"

"My dear Feeney, I have lived down here for a few years. Our Vincent Conway was born in Sea Isle City, the Blaine boys were from Delaware. This case has a seashore ring to it, and I believe the tattoos come part and parcel with it."

Feeney, smiled and shook his head. He looked at Stansfield and said,

"This is why we solved cases, because my mystical partner always came up with these wild ideas, that somehow panned out."

Stansfield,

"I would like to set some ground rules here, and I hope we can all agree. Sean, you have a busy caseload to supervise up in the City. If you can provide Red and me with lab support, and some records checking we can then run the interviews and any leads that come up. Is that acceptable?"

"Red, I like this guy. Sure that would be great, can we plan on having weekly conference calls to see what progress has been made?"

Stansfield,

"That is agreeable, we will keep you informed. Meanwhile, I will be looking into the activities of Patrick Blaine. His father not seeing his son for two years may hold water in a big city, but not in a rural Delaware county."

The meeting ended. Blackman and Feeney departed and talked in the parking lot for a few minutes. Then Feeney headed North, while Blackman went South to Tuckahoe.

# THIRTY-SIX

1987
Niederweningen, Switzerland
Hotel Du Chasseur, 15 Dorfstrasse

H E HAD COME by train from Zurich to meet with the man he knew only by reputation. The hotel room was very comfortable and very bright. He had been told he would be contacted at 2PM, and to stay in his room. With about three hours remaining he took a shower, ordered some lunch from room service, and read a book he had brought with him. At exactly 2PM there was a knock on the locked adjoining room door. He opened his side and was facing a tall man dressed in a suit. The man motioned for him to enter, then requested he raise his arms. He was patted down for weapons, the man gestured for him to talk a seat. Asked if he wanted a drink, he declined, and sat for the next 15 minutes. Then a door opened, and a tall man entered. He extended his hand and said,

"Mr. Ordonez, it's is a pleasure to meet you, my brothers say you are a good and honorable man, my name is Osama bin Laden."

Pedro, shook his hand and responded,

"An honor sir, I have heard a lot about you from our mutual friends."

As both men sat down, bin Laden motioned to his man to get him a whiskey, and anything for his guest. Pedro was surprised and ordered bourbon on ice. His host smiled for he had sensed his surprise.

"I know, Muslims do not drink alcohol, but I acquired the taste in the Royal Saudi court. One must not be constrained by every rule written."

"Yes, it would not be such a fascinating world if we adhered to the old ways."

They talked for the next five minutes about Switzerland when their drinks arrived.

bin Laden,

"I have checked with our mutual friends in North Africa and they say you have paid them fair prices for their product. I have also learned that your markets in Europe are very profitable. I believe you and I can make a business deal that will be most profitable for both of us."

"I am not opposed to listening to your proposal, I have come this far, so please continue."

"Good, may I ask who your source is for heroin?"

"Sulaman Shafiri in Ankara, he has supplied my business for the past five years."

"What if I told you he is on the CIA payroll, and can pose a future problem for you and your firm."

"How do you know this?"

"The Americans talk to the Saudi's, and I listen to the Saudi's, it is a very small world."

Squirming in his seat, Pedro Ordonez knew this would be a threat to his business, so he continued listening to the tall Saudi.

"Through my connections in Afghanistan, I can arrange a new supplier, that will provide on time delivery and a much better grade of quality. Are you interested?"

"At this point I would be a fool not to be interested, but what is in this for you?"

"I need to get my people into Europe and the United States. You already have routes mapped out. I give you the Afghanistan connection, you smuggle my people in."

"How many persons are you talking about?"

"For Europe I will need to get 600 on the continent by this June, and in September we will be sending 600 operators to the United States. For this my organization will pay you $50 million.

"Then I must say I am sorry, for I have not that size of ship that can transit the ocean."

"What if I was to provide you with the proper ships, could you do it?

"I suppose I could then, but where are you going to get such ships?"

"From our common enemy."

"Our common enemy, and who may that be?"

"Seaford Incorporated. I know you have been at war with them for some time. I asked them to help me with this request and they turned me down. Thus, your enemy is my enemy, and you are my friend. I have learned through my Far Eastern sources they are involved in building six ships in South Korea. A common ocean going freighter with a unique interior design, a secret hold that can contain 500 tons. My plan is steal one of these boats, take it to a friendly member state and make some outward changes. With a new name, paint, and silhouette change we can start our European operation."

"You initially said ships, where do we get the other one?

"Seaford has in its employ a Filipino captain who can be bribed with gold. The Seaford ship *Tiger Star* will also be transformed, and re-named. We will then begin our American operation. Pedro, are you onboard for this?"

With a smile and the want to destroy Seaford, Ordonez replied,

"Of course, my new friend."

Both men grabbed their glasses, stood and toasted their new union.

Across the street a directional microphone had been aimed at the hotel room of the meeting. With the meeting ending, the 2-man team gathered up their electronic equipment and packed it away. They left the building in a sedan and headed for their safe house in Zurich. Within a few hours the entire meeting conversation would be analyzed in the underground rooms of the Mossad in Tel Aviv.

THIRTY-SEVEN

1987
Pleasantville, NJ

BLACKMAN HAD ASKED around about tattoo parlors, and from a few good sources he learned Froggy's Tattoos in Pleasantville had the best reputation. Entering the parlor he found several people being worked on. He asked for the owner. A longhaired male wearing a leather vest said he was the owner and would be right with him as soon as he finished his present customer.

Blackman took a seat and waited about ten minutes.

When the owner was finished and his customer paid him, he came over to Blackman. Extending his hand he said,

"I'm Froggy Denworth, how can I help you?

"Nice to meet you Froggy, my name is Red

Blackman. I am not here for a tattoo, but need your expertise in identifying one. Can you help me or point me in the right direction with this."

He pulled out 3 close up photographs of the tattoos from the murders.

"You a cop?"

"Used to be, I retired, now I'm consulting on a case."

Froggy looked at all three photos. He studied each carefully. Then went to his desk and took a magnifying glass from the drawer. Again, he looked at each photo closely.

"This is "old school work", the inking on the anchor is very intense and unique. Matter of fact, it is the same in each photo.

The outer oval is very precise, very good work. I have not seen this before, and I could not tell you who the artist was, but he was a master."

"Do you know of anyone who could identify the artist?"

Froggy thought for several seconds then went to a bookcase. The book was filled with all types of designs. He found one that was from a tat parlor in South Philly called the Reverse Image on Durfur Street.

"This one is the closest to what you have, try this place."

"Thank you very much Froggy, I'll take a trip to Philly."

"Your welcome. One question about those photos, did these guys get caught?"

"No, they were all murdered."

Froggy didn't say anything, he just shook his head as Blackman left the parlor.

Next day, Philadelphia, Pennsylvania

Red found the tattoo parlor at 14 Durfur Street in South Philly. The neighborhood was old and shabby, but there was a people presence on the street. He entered the shop, asked for the manager.

An older man said,

"Who's asking?"

"My name is Blackman, I'm assisting the New Jersey State Police regarding a double murder. Both victims had a specific tattoo on their inner right arms. I was told it looks "old school", and may have come from here.

"Who are you?"

"My name is Tony Maze, let me see what you got."

He took the photos from Blackman, then handed them back.

"This is no work that came out of here, but there was a guy in Philly who may have done this, last I heard of him, he was working biker bars in Jersey."

"Do you have a name?"

"Don't know his real name, but he goes by the name Knucklehead."

"How many biker bars in New Jersey?"

"A lot."

Backman stared down at the floor then said,

"Thank you for your time Tony, I appreciate your time."

"Hey, you got a card, if I hear something maybe I can call you ."

Blackman knew better, now that he was a civilian.

"Just contact the Bass River State Police barracks and asked for Detective Stansfield."

As he left he got into his car, but waited. Within a minute Tony Maze was locking up the storefront, and running to a corner bar. Blackman followed him in, and found him making a call from a pay phone. Blackman had seen an alley outside the bar and waited.

As Maze came by, he grabbed him by the collar and threw him against the wall. As he held him against the wall, he grabbed Maze's crotch and twisted. Maze screamed, then he let up on the pressure.

"Who did you call scumbag, tell me now or you will be singing soprano with the street corner quartet."

There was no answer, just rapid breathing. He twisted harder and Tony was screaming louder.

"Okay, stop, god-dammit stop!"

Blackman stooped, Tony recovered his breath.

"Who did you call?"

"My partner, Dar Zucchino

"Where is he?, no more lying!"

He grabbed Tony, and started squeezing his testicles.

Tony was about to pass out, when Blackman eased up.

"Where is your partner?"

"If I tell you, he is dead!"

Blackman reached into his pocket and pulled out a Smith and Wesson Centennial .38 snub nose. He jammed it into Tony's mouth.

"No your dead, say goodbye!"

Tony's eyes were wide with fear, when he started talking with the gun in his mouth. Blackman pulled the gun, and aimed it at his crotch.

"Talk!"

"He in AC at the Breed's bar.

Blackman never liked lying scumbags, so in a quick swipe with the gun he hit Maze on the chin, who collapsed to the ground. Blackman now had a lead, and he headed back to New Jersey.

CHAPTER THIRTY-EIGHT

1987
HTB Shipbuilders, Geoje Island, South Korea

IT WAS A very informal ships launch. The executives of HTB, now a subsidiary of Seaford Incorporated watched as Andrew Conway handed the bottle of champagne to Abigail Conway Phipps to smash across the hull of the companies newest ship. With a mighty swing she proclaimed,

"I launch the good ship *Abigail Conway*, may she sail the seas with a free spirit, and success!"

As the ship made it way down the ways, an eager crew manned the deck. Andrew smiled, for he knew this first ship would make a lot of money. The next day he and Abigail would fly home, while the ship was fitted out. In another two weeks all the work was completed and the new ship sailed for her first destination.

As she cleared the channel and entered the Korean Straits, a smaller ship followed. Bearing the name, *Bashera Star* the ship contained a twenty-man contingent of armed Al Queda fighters. For the next week she would shadow the Abigail Conway from a safe distance. The Abigail Conway then stopped at the port of Wenzhou in China.

This would be the first loading of cargo into the hidden hold, 200 tons of Fentanyl. The loading only lasted six hours and soon the ship departed for the Philippines. In four days they were tied up to a dock at Olongapo. The hidden hold was opened and 250 tons of weapons were loaded. Counterfeit .45 caliber automatic pistols and six shot Saturday Night Specials in .38 Special caliber made in jungle villages, would flood the US and Mexican gun markets. Then all the remaining holds were filled with Philippine manufactured toys, kitchenware, clothing, and bottled spices. Three days later, the Abigail set sail for Wilmington, North Carolina as her final destination.

The Al Queda boat radioed the information, then pulled away from her quarry. As the ship sailed the Pacific for a Panama Canal transit, Muslim radical allies of Al Queda were on a intercepting course out of Indonesia. The *Cosmos Stellar* was a 1728-ton general cargo ship that would soon be demolished for scrap, but she was perfect for this mission. As the

Abigail Conway plied the sea on a very dark night, they heard an explosion nearby, then fire. Flares went up, and a lifeboat was lowered. The captain of the *Abigail* ordered the ship to slow and give assistance. As the *Abigail* neared the *Cosmos Stellar*, five rigid inflatable boats with outboard motors were on her stern. Using grappling hooks, heavily armed invaders climbed to the main deck of the ship. With the captain and crew concentrating on the people in the lifeboat, they never saw the black masked pirates on their ship. The first one killed was the radio operator, then they surprised the captain on the bridge. The pirates then entered the down passages to the engine room and killed all present. Another group killed all the crew present in the ships quarters and galley. The entire operation was over in ten minutes. Bodies were thrown over the side, and the *Abigail Conway* under a new crew followed the *Cosmos Stellar* back to its port in Indonesia. It took about 2 days sailing for the ships to reach Sorong in West Papua. In a small cove, a shipyard began the transformation of the *Abigail Conway*. She would no longer resemble the ship that was launched. The smokestack was taken down, and replace by two shorter stacks. The bridge roof was removed and built up some two more levels. Bridge windows were changed from square to old oval. The ships radar was changed to an older model, while the entire

ship was repainted. The two lifeboats were replaced
with rafts. In ten days the original *Abigail Conway* had
disappeared, now replaced by a rusty looking cargo
hauler. Registered in Kuala Lumpur she bore the name
Trade Fortune. Money was paid and the documents for
the new ship were legitimized, even a Certificate of
Insurance from Lloyds of London. Back on her course
for the Panama Canal she would offload her regular
cargo at the Dominican Republic port of Barahona.
Pedro Ordonez was there to meet his new ship and
crew. Standing beside him was Captain Arturo Bracos
of the *Tiger Star.* He was there to collect his gold and
arrange for the turnover of his ship to Ordonez. For
the next five days trucks carrying the legitimate cargo
were busy moving it to other ships. Ordonez had sold
it all off to eager buyers. He smiled at the thought of
Seaford losing her cargo to him, and that would pay
for a transformation of the *Tiger Star.* The number
five hold was opened and special care was given to the
Fentynyl. Pedro would keep this for his own networks.
The guns were something he did not want anything to
do with so they were placed on a barge and dumped it
into the sea. A pickup truck arrived and four men unloaded a crate and placed in on the dock at the feet of
Captain Bracos. The crate contained twenty-five bars
of gold bullion worth some one hundred thousand
dollars each. Bracos would never be seen again as he

left for parts unknown away from the far reaching eyes of Seaford. The Ordonez Cartel now with two ships would soon begin the transit of Al Queda operators into Europe and the United States courtesy of Seaford International.

THIRTY-NINE

1987
New Seaford Corporation, NJ

THE NEWS HIT Andrew Conway like a sledgehammer. His new ship hadn't checked in with the corporation's maritime section. She was expected to be at the Pacific entrance of the Panama Canal tomorrow, but no reports on her present location. He ordered his people to check all Pacific sources for any sightings, all coming back negative. Unbeknownst to him, the ship had been hijacked, and was now undergoing a transformation. Andrew checked the ships manifest, and went right to a coded page that specified the contents of Hold #5. 200 tons of Fentanyl with a street value of billions of dollars was catastrophic, the guns would have yielded at least $10 million dollars, plus the possible loss of the ship was searing. Seaford was being attacked by outside forces. He had to find out who they were, and destroy them. As he pondered this new problem his head of maritime operations called to report that *Tiger Star* was not in communication with headquarters and had failed to call in on a weekly check. This was not coincidence but a planned overt act against Seaford.

First, he issued orders to his maritime division to report the *Abigail Conway* missing, this would commence a search and rescue mission Pacific wide. Second, Seaford would alert Lloyds of London so as to recoup some of the loss.

Third, call in the family elites and have then make inquiries behind the scene with foreign acquaintances.

Fourth, put out the word amongst the underworld, that Seaford will pay top dollar for information regarding the location and sale of the Fentanyl and the guns. And lastly, he needed a man; he could trust and be his assassin when he found the thieves. Going to his wall safe he pulled out an old leather pocket book that contained many phone numbers. He dialed the international operator and placed a call to the Island of Sardinia. A male voice answered the phone.

"Hello"

"Hector, this is Andrew Conway, we need to meet.

"Two days from now, 3PM by the Spanish Steps in Rome."

Then he hung up the phone. Andrew called his secretary to get him on a Rome flight tomorrow

CHAPTER FORTY

1987
Milford, Delaware
Milford Police Department

DAN STANSFIELD INTRODUCED himself to the desk officer, and waited for the Chief. Moments later a man came out and introduced himself a Chief Jack Gallagher. Stansfield presented his credentials.

"Chief, I'm investigating a double homicide in Jersey. Both victims were brothers from Delaware. Brother number one worked for his family's company in Holt's Neck. Company is called DelMarVa Ship and Tool. Brother number two lived her in Milford. His name was Patrick Blaine. I need to know if your department ever had any dealings with him."

"Detective, why don't we go back to my office."

The Chief led him into a brightly lit office, and

closed the door. He then sat down behind his desk. He went to his computer and entered the name Patrick Blaine. Soon the screen showed some incidents.

July 4, 1986 Public Intoxication- fined $100

November 15, 1986 Ran a red light – fined $75.00

"That's all we have on him. Nothing stands out that makes him a public enemy."

"Do you have a place of work, or his profession?"

"Stated he was a commercial fisherman, crewed the *Sea Traveler* out of Cape Henlopen."

"Guess, I'll run down to the Cape and talk to them, thank you for your time Chief Gallagher."

"Well it was good to meet you, if you need anything else give me a call."

As Stansfield left, the Chief waited and watched. When he saw Stansfield car leaving the parking lot, he placed a call to his brother-in-law Ralph Blaine.

"Hello DelMarVa Ship and Tool."

"Ralph, this is Jack, just had a NJ State Police Detective Stansfield here asking about Patrick."

"What did you tell him?"

"I showed him the made up police record we concocted."

"Did he buy it?"

"I think so, sent him over to the *Sea Traveller*, he should be there in about 30 minutes."

"Well the ship is out fishing, but I'll alert my sister, she'll say the right words."

Ralph hung up and called the *Sea Traveller* office. "Hello."

"Eileen, there is a Jersey State cop coming your way asking about Patrick, you know what to say."

"Ok, Ralph, I'll take care of it."

Conversation ended, she waited for the cops arrival.

It started to rain when she saw headlights enter the property. A single person exited the car and came to the office door and rang the bell. She got up and opened the door. Stansfield showed her his badge and ID. She invited him inside. She extended her hand to him.

"I'm Eileen Grayson, my husband and I own the trawler *Sea Traveller* how can I help you?"

"I'm investigating the homicide of one Patrick Blaine. I have learned he was commercial fisherman and crewed your boat. Did you know him?

"Yes, I did, he worked for us for about 2 years. Good worker, had no problems with him. He was a nice guy, I was shocked when I heard he had been murdered."

"Is there anyone else who worked with him."

"Yes, my husband Norman, he's captain of the *Sea Traveler.*"

"Is he here."

"Right now he is on the boat fishing. Been gone for five days and will return hopefully with a full catch of cod."

"How long has this business in your family?

"Oh we've been fishing for over seventy years, my grandfather owned the first *Sea Traveller*."

"Well thank you very much Mrs. Grayson, I think I have enough information, no need to further bother you, thank you for your time."

"You weren't a bother Detective, good luck."

As Stansfield left, he noticed a wall of pictures with people and fish. One caught his eye. He turned and asked,

"Wow, I would have loved to have caught that one, how many pounds was that?

She came over, and looked at the photo. She smiled and said,

"650 lb. Bluefin tuna, that's my father. He caught him on the *Sea Traveller 2* back in the sixties."

Stansfield smiled, and just shook his head.

"What a fish, he must have battled that one?"

"Sure did, took him about 5 hours to land him."

Stansfield waved his hand goodbye and left the office, not thinking about the fish, but the fisherman in the photo with the oval and anchor tattoo on his inner right arm.

CHAPTER FORTY-ONE

1987
Rome, Italy
The Spanish Steps 3PM

ANDREW CONWAY ARRIVED about a minute before three. He was holding a tourist brochure and one thought he was looking at the Steps, but his eyes moved all around. He spotted the man he was there to meet. As the man came by, they silently nodded, and the man continued on. Andrew waited for twenty seconds then followed him. He must have walked two blocks when he entered a small hotel. As Andrew entered the lobby he did not see him, but this was pre-arranged. He went over to the desk and gave his name as Senor Rossatto. The clerk handed him a room key marked 814. Taking the elevator to the eighth floor, he went right and found room 814 at the end of the hallway. Opening the door he entered and heard the click of a hammer on a gun. Seated was the man he had followed from the Steps. The man got up and they shook hands. Hector, had an eye condition known as Nevus of Ota, a birthmark that covered the white part of his left eye.

"I am glad to see you Andrew, it looks life has been good to you and your family."

"Yes, Hector, the family is fine, but I am having a problem with some of my operations. I need you and your group to find out who is interfering.

"We have done business in the past, and my people always have their ears to the ground, any movement in our worlds will be noticed. So start at the beginning."

For the next hour Andrew told Hector about his hijacked cocaine shipment and the murder of the two cousins, the Brooklyn warehouse being torched, and the missing ships and cargo.

"I must ask you this Andrew, who are these enemies of yours, certainly you must have some idea?"

"I cannot think of anyone. Yes, thru the years we have dealt severely with those who have intruded on our family and company, but I cannot think of anyone or group that has declared war on us."

"Have you refused anyone the services of your company?"

Andrew thought for a minute, then said,

"I had a request to smuggle in Muslim terrorists to Europe and the US on my new ships, but I refused."

"Who made this request for the Muslims?"

"He said his name was bin Laden, and they would pay any amount to get their people across borders."

Hector eyes went wide when he heard the name.

"Osama bin Laden is a very serious man, he is most powerful amongst the Muslims. In your refusal you may have created a new enemy."

"Hector, whatever it takes, someone has stolen from my family, they have killed family members, and if it is this bin Laden, I need to know. Will you take this on?"

"This will be more expensive than my previous jobs, are you prepared for that?"

"I want to know who is involved, find that out and give me the proof, cost is not a factor."

"Well our business is concluded, do have a nice return trip. I will keep you posted on our progress, my friend."

"Thank you Hector, I know you will be successful."

CHAPTER FORTY-TWO

1987

N.J. State Police Barracks Bass River

THE TELECONFERENCE BEGAN with Stansfield telling about his discovery in Delaware.

"Red was right, these cases have a shore flavor and smell. I believe we need to look into relationships down here. That photo I saw was in the sixties. We may need to go back further in time."

Feeney,

"I have a friend in the Two-Six, they just broke a big stock swindle researching family trees of the perpetrators. Maybe we should think of using that technique?"

Blackman,

"We have the names of the victims and birthdates. In all the cases we know the names of the parents, and now we have a name of this woman in Delaware. Let's get some experts on this one. Sean, find out who your friend used, and get them on board."

"Will do Red."

"Now, I have this lead on a tattoo artist holed up with the Breed in Atlantic City. I will be going there see what this guy has to say."

Stansfield,

"Good idea Red, but not without some muscle. I know this gang, and they may be trouble. I will arrange for some troopers to be with you when you go into that bar."

"Ok Dan, this may be interesting."

Feeney,

"You know, maybe a little action will get the rust off of him."

"Look who's talking, the last action you had was sending out your support checks to your ex-wives!"

You could hear Feeney laughing; Stansfield smiled and just shook his head.

CHAPTER FORTY-THREE

1987
Wolford's Bar,
Drexel Avenue, Atlantic City, NJ

IT WAS THE beginning of the Christmas Season that changed the décor of this dive bar. A string of lights was strung around the main room, and a small Christmas tree was over by the jukebox. There was a room off the main area that housed a tattoo parlor. A small plastic Santa Claus waved to everyone. The bartender had a two foot long braided pig-tail and both arms heavily tattooed. At the bar were about seven Breed members sitting and drinking, and wearing their "colors". Red Blackman walked in, and took a seat at the bar. The bartender announced,

"This is a members only bar, you'll have to leave."

"Well, I'm not here to become a member, I am looking for Dar Zucchino, is he around?"

One of the members seated at the bar looked at Blackman.

"You look like a cop. We don't like cops."

"Well I was a cop, but I'm retired, and guess what? I like cops. Just tell me where Dar is and I will be out of here."

"What if we don't tell you, what are you going to do, arrest us?"

"No, but they will."

The door opened and in walked two uniformed NJ State Troopers. Both were about 6'6" and probably tipped the scales at a muscular 285.

The boys at the bar stopped talking, and stared as the two backed up Blackman. Then they heard a door slam from the area of the tattoo parlor. The bartender smiled and said,

"You'll have to find him somewhere else."

"No. I don't think so."

The main door opened and another big trooper appeared clutching a scraggly bearded man with many tattoos.

"Caught him in the alley, is this the guy?"

"Sure is Trooper, he and I just need to sit down to talk?"

The three troopers had the bartender come out from behind the bar and take a seat with the club members.

One of them said.

"Now you tough little boys continue to drink, and let our friend do his job. We'll make sure you all don't interfere."

With Zucchino sitting at a table, Blackman took a chair and sat down.

"Had a hard time trying to find you, understand you think someone will kill you, why is that?"

Zucchino just stared across the room.

Blackman then took out the three photographs and laid them on the table.

"Who did these tattoos?

Zucchino finally spoke,

"If I tell you, I'm dead!"

"Look, we have three guys with this same tat dead, and l want to know?

There was shock on his face.

"They're dead."

"As cold as ice. Now who did these tattoos?

"I did, I was trained by a master, who was trained by the master who started it all."

"So what happened to these masters?

"They all passed away, from natural causes."

"So why do you think someone will kill you?

"The tat, the master must never divulge their identity, or he will die.

"Is that why you're here with the Breed, for protection?"

"Yes, they can't find me here, but you did."

"Can I call you Dar?

He nodded yes.

"Dar, I need to take you to a place where we can talk, you'll be safe. Help us out, answer some questions and I promise your back here within a day. If that is agreeable, just nod yes."

He did.

"Okay, you and I are going to get up, go over to the bar and you tell your friends your going with us. All we want to do is talk you, your not being charged with anything."

Dar, went over to the bar, and spoke with the bartender and one of the Breed. The conversation lasted about five minutes, when they patted him on his back and he turned and walked over to Blackman. The three big troopers followed them out. In a few minutes they were on their way to the Bass River barracks.

FORTY-FOUR

1987
Manhattan North Homicide, NYPD

L T. SEAN FEENEY went into the conference room to meet the person who had come highly recommended from his friend in the Two-Six. Seated was a female, nicely dressed, and very attractive. She stood up and introduced herself as Sharon Olsen. Feeney shook her hand, noticing the Rolex Oyster watch on her wrist, and a wedding band on left hand. The gold chain around her neck was very real as well as her diamond stud earrings. He began,

"Our mutual friend Charlie Bauer at the Two-Six was highly appreciative of your help, where did you come by this experience?"

"I have a degree in Forensic Science from John Jay. Was hired by the Pennsylvania State Police, worked in their lab for about ten years. Met an architect, fell in love, got married, had some kids. He became a partner in a large NYC firm, and we have a house in Westchester. Started researching my family tree and got real interested in the subject. A friend of mine knew Charlie, he contacted me to help him out. I got the info he needed, and the rest is history."

"Well, Charlie certainly got a lot of arrests and indictments. You obviously did a good job."

"Thank you Lieutenant, it was very satisfying to be part of that case."

"I am going to tell you a story that started with a murder in the South Bronx in 1968, do you have the time to listen?"

"I'm listening."

For the next hour and a half he related the Vinny Conway Jr. murder right up to the co-investigation with the NJ State Investigation regarding the murder of the Blaine Brothers.

"Mrs. Olsen, now you know what we have. We need your expertise to determine if these cases have a "family thread" that will lead us to the killers. We need everything you can gather on these people including financials, legal cases, as well as the family history. Are you game?"

"Lieutenant Feeney, first off, call me Sharon. And yes, I believe I can help you and your friends in Jersey."

"Alright Sharon, give me your e-mail address and I will forward the necessary paperwork and information. Also, here is a number we use for teleconferencing, when the team meets.

"Thanks, happy to be aboard, tell me who are your partners in Jersey."

"State Police Detective Dan Stansfield, and my ex-partner Red Blackman, who is a civilian consultant down there."

Olsen began to smile.

"What's so funny?"

"I just put it together. Going to John Jay we heard of two wild guys in the Bronx with an amazing case closing record. Your Beer, aren't you?"

Feeney was smiling, and nodded yes.

Olsen,

"And Bagels he's in Jersey? Well I can't wait to meet him?

"Sharon, I was the smarter one of that duo."

She laughed and laughed.

CHAPTER FORTY-FIVE

1987
NJ State Police Barracks, Bass River

SEATED ROUND THE table were Blackman, Stansfield and Zucchino. The ink artist was more relaxed as he drank his coffee and smoked a cigarette.

Blackman,

"Dar, in AC you mentioned the word, "Masters", who were they?

"I was told it all started with a whaling sailor named Josiah Webster. He was from Portsmouth, New Hampshire and crewed whaling ships that sailed the world. On one cruise, his ship the *Elizabeth Kay* struck a reef and sank. All hands were lost, except Josiah who was rescued and taken to Japan. There he recuperated, but stayed. He loved the Japanese culture and married.

His father-in-law was a master tattoo artist, and it was there he learned to be a master. The Japanese ink masters are the crème de la crème of their art; the colors and work are the best. After 20 years his wife died, so Josiah came back to the United States. I was told it was in the year 1903 that he settled in Maryland on the Eastern Shore. He bought a small farm in Taylorville. Soon word got put that he was a master of the black ink, and sailors would come to his farm. Around 1918 a maritime man came to him with an idea for a tattoo, and Josiah completed it. This man was very wealthy and his offer to Josiah was to come to New Jersey and work for him. He was happy with his farm, but this man made him an offer beyond his wildest dreams. Josiah sold his farm to the man at a big profit, went to New Jersey and was given land on this man's land for free. He could farm his land, and sell his produce to the markets. All he had to do was to be available to draw the same tattoo for the man's entire family. Josiah lived to 1939, he was buried on his land in New Jersey. He had an apprentice named Mario Christaldi. Mario started as a farm hand for Josiah, but eventually became the master's apprentice. Mario took over the farm, and married. They had a daughter born in 1942 and a son born in 1948 he died in Vietnam. The daughter married my father Ray Zucchino. My grandfather trained me and I became a master of black ink with one family of clients. I lived at my grandfather's farm, until he died in 1982. I became part owner of a tat parlor in Philly, got into drugs and ran away from life. For the last 3 years I travelled the world as a common seaman, fry cook, farmhand, and thief. The family that used my grandfather's services put a bounty out for me, but they never found me. I took the protection of the Breed until you found me."

Stansfield,

"What is the name of the family that has used your services and now has a bounty on you?"

Without hesitation Zucchino answered,

"Conway."

Blackman,

"What about Blaine?"

"Wouldn't know that name, everyone was always Mr. Conway. You would get a phone call the day before that someone was coming for a tattoo at a certain time the next day. The next day a person would show up at the farmhouse and get the tattoo. Always the same tat, the Oval and Anchor. Talking was forbidden, it only took 40 minutes to complete the tat. They would put down an envelope containing three thousand dollars and leave. Some months 4 tats, another month 2 tats, it varied."

Blackman pulled out a photo of the face of Vincent Conway Jr.,

"Did you ever see this guy?"

Zucchino studied the photo and said,

"Oh yeah, he drove up in an expensive car, seemed like he was in a rush."

Then they showed him the photos of the Blaine brothers.

"I remember this guy, he showed before the other guy."

It was Patrick Blaine's photo.

"Came in a pickup truck, smoked about five cigarettes.

The other guy also drove a pickup truck. What I remember of him was that he was the first one ever to say thank you for the tat."

Stansfield looked at Blackman, the Oval and Anchor was no longer a mystery. The Conway family was a part of puzzle now exposed. Now if Sean Feeney and his new source could reveal more evidence, they could piece it all together.

Blackman,

"Did you ever hear or see anything that could give a specific name of the individuals that showed?'

"No, just a Mister Conway was coming, do the tat and get your money."

"Dar, you have been a great help. As I said before we are not charging you with anything. A car will take you back to AC."

Zucchino got up and shook hands with Blackman and Stansfield. You could see he was relieved.

Stansfield escorted him out to the waiting car.

FORTY-SIX

1988
The Port of Toulon, France

To ANDREW CONWAY he was known as Hector, but his real name was Paolo Sassari. His family could be traced back to the 15th Century in Sardinia. They were professional mercenaries and assassins that had worked for the Vatican, the Borgia's, and heads of state, and international corporations. Paolo's business gave him entry into areas where others would or could not tread. He was wired into the underworld, and he was a master of how it all worked. The missing Seaford boats were easily located and identified. The former *Abigail Conway* was now named the *Trade Fortune* and was now under surveillance in Tripoli, Libya. The former *Tiger Star* was in her last week of transformation at the shipyard in West Papua. She would sail under the new name *Stella Nova*. Paolo's sources told him she was being readied for a stop at Yanbu, Saudi Arabia and then a passage thru the Suez Canal. He would not notify Seaford of his findings until he found out who now operated the boats. Experience had shown him to allow the prey a sense of freedom. They will begin to think nobody else knows. His agents would follow and report back. Upon reaching their destinations, the money would be exchanged, and that will be when the prey is fully exposed.

FORTY-SEVEN

1988
Briarcliff Manor, NY

OVERLOOKING THE HUDSON River Sharon Olsen was in her home office. Her architect husband Richard, had designed this space with her input. Her computer area was elevated and faced a very large window that could view the river and see the Ramapo Mountains. As she settled in her investigation of family Conway, all the information forwarded by Feeney was put into her online mixing bowl. With some 15 different search engines all dedicated to Ancestry searches, she was able to start plotting the development of the family. Feeney had also asked if she could discover ownerships, properties and tax information. Sharon, had some time ago made connections with a computer programming genius by the name of Alex Sockolof.

He was a professor of business systems at Columbia University. He gave her his latest program, Holly-Lane 8. This program could take a persons name and date of birth, and show their income and ownership of properties and businesses along with the names of partners and associates. Soon she would put this to good use. As she left all the engines and systems working, she only hoped that her efforts would prove fruitful. She enjoyed the thrill of the hunt, and working with the likes of the famous Bagels and Beer duo only enhanced that thrill. As the data started to spew out, she knew that each page required her to sift thru and separate the wheat from the chaff. Her long night began with the first solid name, William Conway in the late 1700's. A family was started and soon sons and daughters began to branch out from the main trunk. Small towns and village names in South Jersey began to appear like Thimbletown, Waretown and Heislerville. The names of ships and farm locations soon were listed. Marriages and new family names evolved like the Blaines and Thompsons. An Alvin William Conway had graduated from the US Naval Academy in 1887. Alvin's naval career had flourished as he retired the Admiral of the Atlantic Fleet in 1916. Several Blaines and Thompsons served in government as congressman and senators. In 1917 the name Roger Conway became prominent with The Conway Company name change to Seaford International. Olsen took this information and put it on the Sockolof search engine. From the 1920's onto the present time Seaford International was a very profitable company. Soon a listing of properties, ships, and businesses was generated. This was a privately held corporation that made huge amounts of money. Whatever financial credit it had was with banks it owned and run by relatives. The listings were numerous and the computer program uncovered every detail. DelMarVa Ship and Tool, and even the *Sea Traveller* fishing vessel made the list. Her ancestral search began to show the relationships and a family tree was constructed with William Conway arriving in 1775 to the marriage of one Nicholas Thompson to Amy Saunders in Rehoboth Beach this past spring of 1987. The computers rolled out more information until the next day. Olsen looked it over, and her thought was how intricate were the ways and methods Seaford International conducted their business. Satisfied, she had completed her assigned task she placed a call to Sean Feeney.

"Sean, Sharon Olsen, I have everything you and your team need to proceed further."

"How long did it take?"

"Almost two straight days, this family has a lot of wealth with many sources of income."

"Look, are you available to meet me tomorrow at Manhattan North?"

"Sure what time?"

"Meet me at 9AM, we will be travelling down to South Jersey. You're going to meet Stansfield and Blackman to go over your findings."

"Ok Sean, see you in the morning."

Feeney then called Stansfield at Bass River.

"Dan, Sharon Olsen called, she did the ancestral search, and a financial search, she came up big. We will be leaving the city at 9AM tomorrow for your place, need to meet with you and Red."

"Red is sitting next to me, I'll put you on speaker."

Blackman,

"What's up, you got something?"

"She uncovered a lot of financial and personal information that may answer some of our prime questions."

"Well you did real good in picking her, it was great move despite the person who thought of it."

"You know Bagels, I am reminded working with you again is such a joy."

"Oh, you know I love you Monsignor."

Feeney smiled,

"And I will keep you in my daily prayers my son."

CHAPTER FORTY-EIGHT

1988
Genoa, Italy

THE *TRADE FORTUNE* outbound from Tripoli arrived in Genoa after some 4 days of sailing. At the dock she unloaded her cargo of gypsum from her visible holds. Undergoing a customs check, she was declared empty and the crew was given a 48-hour layover before the next sailing. On the second night at approximately 10PM, three single straight body trucks pulled up next to the ship. The hidden hold was opened. Seventeen people were seen exiting the ship and getting into the back of a truck, which immediately sped away. The ship's crane started up and soon three pallets of covered material were loaded into the second truck. These were guns and ammunition, explosives, and detonation devices. The cranes again lifted about 4 pallets of Fentanyl and loaded that into the last truck. The trucks left, and soon the dock was very quiet again as silence engulfed the night. The peering eyes that watched the night operation, knew the next act, the wait for the money. In about 2 hours a Maserati bearing two persons pulls up outside the gangway, and a single person exits carrying a briefcase. Eyes watch as the person is seen entering the bridge and meeting a single person. A telescopic lens takes the photo of the Captain. The messenger is allowed to leave, and the observers remain waiting. As the sun rises, a single figure comes down the gangway holding a briefcase and is picked up by a taxi. The taxi is followed into central Genoa. The occupant of the taxi is the Captain of the *Trade Fortune*. He gets out on the corner of Via De Centro and Via della Cella. At number 239 Via De Centro, he goes into a very large office-building lobby filled with people. Followed onto an elevator he presses the button for the 12th Floor. He and three others get off, and he is observed entering a suite of offices marked Consuelo Imports Limited. No less than three minutes inside, he is leaving minus the briefcase. A phone call is put thru to Toulon, and the caller is instructed to stop the surveillance. Of the seventeen Al Queda operatives that exited the *Trade Fortune*, 13 will disperse to various points of the European continent. Four Libyans will take a flight to

Frankfurt, Germany and find a safe house. They will settle in for the coming months. Two will get jobs at the airport, while the other two construct a bomb. On a day in December, a bomb will be strategically placed inside the cargo hold of Pan Am Flight 103. 270 souls will lose their lives over Lockerbie, Scotland. A Libyan connection will be established, yet only to the ones in the know, knew Bin laden had been the trainer.

CHAPTER FORTY-NINE

1988
NJ State Police Barracks, Bass River

THIS WAS THE first time that Sharon Olsen met the team. Dan Stansfield shook her hand, smiled and welcomed her to the New Jersey. Red Blackman took her hand and said motioning toward Feeney.

"I very glad you made it here alive, he is the world's worst driver."

Feeney smiled and said,

"If I was that bad, how come I always drove?"

They were all smiling. As they entered the conference room Stansfield introduced them all to State Police Video Technician Tom Baylor.

"I brought Tom in on this to record this presentation. From what I gather Mrs. Olsen has uncovered some very important information. It is because of that

THE ANCHOR IN THE OVAL 169

information, we need to record it for possible use in the future. Sharon anytime your ready."

"Thank you, in my first meeting with Lieutenant Feeney he related the story of this investigation. From when Vincent Conway Jr. was killed in the Bronx, the massacre at Brown Place, the body that fell from the sky in Dorothy, to the body that washed up in Monmouth County. I was intrigued, and hope to help you with my findings. You determined to look into the relationships, if there were any, and see if something could be developed. In my investigation that I will reveal to you today, I believe the victims were all members of a criminal family that has evolved in the South Jersey area from as far back as the 1700's. Let's start in 1775 when William Conway comes from England as an indentured servant for a colonial American farmer. He worked off his debt and was free to live in Colonial America. Before I start on his future family, William appears to be the only honest one, from here on his sons and daughters take his successful business to new levels and vastly improve upon it by getting into smuggling and other crimes. The Conway family is bolstered thru marriages by the names of Blaine and Thompson. There appears to be two very distinct divisions amongst this family enterprise. The Conway Company involved in smuggling, land ownership, shipping, drugs and political corruption employs all family members in its activities. The educated amongst the Conway, Blaine and Thompson sector rose to seats of power and prominence in politics, government, military, and the corporate world. It appears that these positions suited Conway Company's rise of power. In 1907 The Conway Company became Seaford International and it was here the power and vision of one-man began, Roger Conway."

Blackman,

"May I interrupt? Did you just say Seaford International?"

Olsen,

"Yes, that was new name of The Conway Company."

"Please excuse me again Sharon. "

He spoke to Feeney,

"Sean, when we went to Brooklyn to investigate the parking ticket we found in Vincent Conway's apartment, that no parking zone was in front of a building that said Seaford International."

Feeney,

"I remember our trip to Brooklyn, but don't remember that building. Maybe we should take another trip?"

"No chance, it was burned to the ground. Sharon, please continue."

"Under the stewardship of Roger Conway, Seaford International got into the liquor business and supplied the mob thru offshore and Canadian locations during Prohibition. Heroin became a main source of income with connections straight from Asia. Legitimate sources such as shipping and land ownership also brought in huge amounts of money. Roger turned over control to his son Reggie. Reggie was ruthless, never investigated or arrested, yet during his time Seaford International flourished. Today it is known as New Seaford International with a corporate office in Northfield, NJ Reggie's son Andrew is the CEO. They have many existing contracts with the casino industry, and supply the Atlantic Coast region with everything from gaming tables to landscaping services. In my research I came up with specific names and found them as principles in regard to DelMarVa Ship and Tool, and the Sea Traveller Fishing Company. In 1948 Seaford International was involved in a court case that was decided in their favor by the influence of a US Senator named Blaine, and a presiding Federal judge named Thompson. Seaford was able to take control of a company that manufactured marine equipment, Altus Seapower. Later on a defense contract won by Altus yielded Seaford some $2.5 billion. Resisting any outside takeovers, Seaford is a privately held corporation that is self-insured and worth that some estimate to be $7 billion. Andrew Conway maintains a very low profile. He is married and has three children. He has two brothers, both twins and a younger sister all involved in the workings of the corporation. Andrew was a former Army Ranger officer before joining the company. The corporation is legally represented by the firm of Conway, Stoddard and Daniels, Philadelphia."

Feeney,

"We're familiar with one of the partners."

"Seaford recently bought the South Korean ship-building firm, HTB for $2.5 billion and had a new freighter built for the company., the Abigail Conway. Five more ships are planned. This is a versatile class ship with blue water capabilities all over the world. In South Jersey alone they own some fifty properties from homes, farms, and ship repair yards. In Delaware, they own some 35 properties ranging from homes, boats and ship repair, and a trucking company. In closing, a somewhat invisible empire that makes a lot of money for a small group of people. Any questions?"

Stansfield,

"Sharon, did you come across any banking accounts?"

"Yes, the Cayman Islands and the Channel Islands."

Blackman,

"You said Andrew Conway had a military back-ground, how long in the Army?"

Referring to her notes,

"Andrew graduated The Citadel, got his commission

as an infantry officer, then Ranger training. He served one tour in Vietnam, received a Silver Star, and then resigned his commission."

Feeney,

"Red and I were there at Brown Place after the massacre, that took planning and execution. I got a feeling Andrew was the brains behind it."

Blackman,

"They came in fast and had every angle covered. I think you may be right on that one partner."

Stansfield,

"Sharon speaking for all here, we would like for you to join our group, are you on board?"

"Definitely."

Blackman,

"Ok, so who is killed the Blaine brothers? We know the Toros were responsible for Vincent Conway Jr., and the Toros were massacred. Someone burned down the Brooklyn warehouse, and maybe that same someone murdered the brothers, but why?

Stansfield,

"Revenge is a good motive."

Olsen,

"And why not, if I was a surviving Toro I would seek revenge."

Feeney,

"Do we know if the Toros are still active?

Olsen,

"I can try and find out. If they are, then they have motive to attack Seaford."

Stansfield,

"Proceed on that tact, meanwhile we need to determine what Seaford is really covering up. Ralph Blaine down in Delaware and the whole DelMarVA Ship and Tool operation bear investigating. Red can you start looking into this, my face is known down there.

Blackman,

"You got it Dan. I got a suspicion that maybe we ought to get some idea on the scope of Seaford international bank accounts offshore and in Europe may be a sign of other illegal activities. Sean, you still have contacts with the FBI and Interpol?"

Feeney,

"Yes, some very good people who can help and get the right information."

Stansfield,

"I have some hooks into the Coast Guard and Customs, will be checking on the movements of the Seaford ships maybe we will get lucky. Thanks everybody, welcome Sharon to the crew, and we will meet again in a few weeks."

CHAPTER FIFTY

1988
Port of Yanbu, Saudi Arabia

THE *MV STELLA* *Nova* (former *Tiger Star*) tied up to the pier for loading. Taking on processed fruits, hemp, and several automobiles, her holds were full. The tides were not running for the ship to leave, so she remained pier side till the next morning. There was enough time for her take on some twenty persons and crates later on in the early morning hours. Now secreted in her secret hold she set sail for stops in Athens, Naples and her final stop Antwerp. From a building facing the ship, Hector's people had set up and photographed the movements. The captain was photographed as well as the new passengers, and the loading of the secret hold. A call to Hector was made and everyone was instructed to leave Yanbu and set up in Athens.

FIFTY-ONE

1988
United States Coast Guard, Cape May, NJ

TOM NEWCOMB PICKED up the phone and answered. "Captain Newcomb, OSE."

"Tom, Dan Stansfield, how have you been?"

"Dan, been a long time. What can I do for you?"

"Tom, involved in a triple murder investigation with a South Jersey connection. If I give you some names, can you run them against your database and see what pops up."

"Sure, can do."

Stansfield,

"Seaford Corporation, DelMarVa Ship and Repair, Fishing vessel *Sea Traveller*, Ralph Blaine, Patrick Blaine, Timothy Blaine, Eileen Grayson, *MV Abigail*

Conway, MV Tiger Star, family name Thompson, and Andrew Conway. Anything you have I'll take."

"Dan, we'll start a search and I will call Bass River when I'm finished."

"Thanks Tom, much appreciated."

Newcomb called in his yeoman and gave him the listing,

"Start a database search on these names. When finished my attention only."

"Aye, aye Sir."

OSE stood for Ocean Surveillance East. Not readily known about to the general public, it was a Coast Guard "black" program. Very key to the nation's defense, it existed as a black budget item from the Pentagon and reported directly to the Joint Chiefs of Staff. Millions of dollars of expensive satellite surveillance systems provided a network for the United States to monitor all the sea traffic sailing the oceans to the east of the Continental United States including the Mediterranean Sea. Anything that moved on these waters was tracked. Newcomb, who had 16 years of sea command experience, was the head of this unit. On the west coast was his exact counterpart OSW who monitored the entire Pacific and Indian Oceans. Located in a 3-story office building the OSE blended in with the surrounding Coast Guard operations at Cape May. Newcomb had worked with Dan Stansfield several times in the past, and Stansfield was one of the good guys you could trust, OSE would come thru.

FIFTY-TWO

1988
Briarcliff Manor, NY

USING THE HOLLY Lane 8 programs, Sharon Olsen placed the name of Ordonez into the query. Within an hour results were soon printing out. A company by the name of Consuelo Imports with offices in Banao, Dominican Republic and Genoa, Italy was uncovered. CEO was one Pedro Ordonez. Graduate of the University of Madrid, he had built a company into an international importer. The dates of his taken the reins of Consuelo coincided within a month of the Brown Place massacre. The report mentioned he had two older brothers, both deceased. His company was worth about two billion dollars. Assets included two ocean freighters: The Stella Nova and the Trade Fortune with homeports in Tripoli and Genoa. A check of her customer log showed small international concerns all over the world. Consuelo Imports had interests in Guatemalan coffee, Costa Rican bananas, Saudi Arabian fruits, and Malaysian coconut oil. Privately held with corporate banking accounts in Switzerland and Saint Kitts/Nevis. For all intents and purposes Pedro Ordonez and his company looked legit. Yet, it appeared like a company with no negatives, but it had a past history with a drug gang, and that was why Olsen proceeded further. The Swiss bank accounts would be hard to break into, but the St. Kitts bank would be like opening a tin can for one of her search engines. Putting in the Consuelo Imports name she quickly had the banking records for the past year. The month of July caught her eye. A $50 million deposit had been made that month, surely unusual from the other months where the average deposit ranged from a million to three million dollars a month. Further checking showed it was a wire transfer from the Bank of Riyadh. The transfer information revealed it was from the account of the Saudi Arabian Construction LLC of Riyadh. With this new information she queried about the Saudi company. Information came back that no such company existed.

CHAPTER FIFTY- THREE

1988
Athens, Greece

T IED TO A pier in Athens, the *MV Stella Nova* unloaded some of her Tripoli cargo. With a schedule
to leave for Naples by dawn, no one saw the three persons leave the ship carrying sea bags. They all rented
rooms in a small hotel near the Flisvous Marina. The
next morning with a car provided for their objective,
2 of men drove the car to a pier. The *City of Poros*, a
small island cruise ship was their target. With bombs
set to detonate they were going to drive the car over
the pier onto the ship.

A premature explosion happened, the car and its
occupants blew up on the pier. With the ship intact, the
local police did not connect the car explosion to terrorism. In a few hours the ship was boarding passengers.

The last member of the team went on board and when the ship was underway, he came forth with a AK-47 and grenades. Killing some 11 persons in the first 2 minutes, he attempted to detonate his suicide vest, but it failed. An armed ship's officer fired his pistol and severely wounded the terrorist. 98 other passengers were injured. All members of this team were Palestinian and trained by Al Queda. Very few intelligence agencies took note for most could not connect this incident to Al Queda because they had never heard of it, or even knew of the widespread influence of Osama bin Laden. Those that were interested began to take note. Hector now made his call to Andrew Conway.

"I have the information you need."

"Shall we meet at our secondary location?"

"I will be there in three days, let us say 1PM."

Conway.

"Very good, 1PM."

CHAPTER FIFTY- FOUR

1988
Manhattan North Precinct, NYPD

SEAN FEENEY WAS calling in all his markers. His first call was to FBI Special Agent Mike Czarnowski at the FBI, Washington D. C. Headquarters. Czarnowski and Feeney knew each other from the old South Bronx precinct. Mike had gotten his degree in law and left the NYPD for the Bureau. They were always in touch with each other and had worked together on several joint cases. To Feeney, Mike was the only Fed he truly trusted.

"Is this the Polish Prince?"

"Ah, his eminence the Monsignor. How have you been Sean?"

"Busy as always. I'm working a old cold case from the Bronx, that now has surfaced in South Jersey.

I'm working with a good Jersey trooper by the name of Stansfield, and a consultant. We come up with a possible tie in and so far it is becoming international in scope. I could use your help Mikey, can you do it?"

"For you Sean, what do you need?"

"The name of the company is Seaford International, CEO is Andrew Conway. Need to know location of all International banking accounts, and names. This a privately held company, that is worth some $7 Billion. Smuggling and drugs may be the key item, but so far we have 3 dead bodies all related to the CEO. I'll send you a listing of names to check, so see what you can unravel. I'll be calling your Rabbi in Interpol."

"Phillipe will be glad to hear from you. By the way speaking of Rabbis, you heard from Bagels?"

"Who do you think the consultant is in South Jersey."

"Say hello to that maniac, every time I think of him I just shake my head and grin."

"Yeah, he tends to do that to everybody. I'll tell him you said hello."

"Take care Sean."

"Same to you Mikey."

CHAPTER FIFTY-FIVE

1988
Tel Aviv, Israel

TAL BORUSH WASHED his hands at the restroom sink. As he reached for the paper towel he noticed in the mirror that he had some crumbs in his mustache from lunch. Wiping them away, he knew this was going to be a tough day. Going back to his small cubicle he sat down in front of his computer, to continue the project he was working on. As senior analyst for terror intelligence he was going over the incident that happened in Athens, so far some interesting facts. The bodies were never identified of the two in the car that blew up on the dock, however the explosives were identified as Semtex. The single terrorist that did board the ship was identified as a Palestinian, named Rasuli Gfii. He was captured because his suicide

185

vest failed to explode. Now sitting in a Greek prison Gfir resisted interrogation and did not say anything. With the click of his mouse, Borush had two pages of information on Gfir. The Mossad has accumulated this information since the late seventies. As Borush scanned it, he saw that Gfir had flown to Cyprus the previous year and changed planes for Yemen. He did not return for over four months. Upon his return to Israel, he was followed and photographed. Everyday he was followed to his job in Hebron, and each time he returned to his house. As Borush looked at the photos he compared them with a photo of Gfir before he left for Cyprus. He was not the same man in his physical being. He had put on muscle, and apparently had lost weight. His face was thinner and his body was more erect than before. This guy had done some training Borush thought, and he was being groomed for that mission in Athens. So what happened in Yemen, and where? Borush wrote it down to be pushed up for consideration by the Director. He was not finished, how did Gfir get to Athens? He would check all the airlines and ships arrivals a month before the incident. The Mossad's computers were the most comprehensive collection of data in the spy business. It would be a few hours for that request to be answered. Borush got up from his desk, left the building and walked to the Tel Aviv beach where the sun and beautiful bikinied women were in large supply. As he sat at a café table he ordered a beer and watched the world go by. Once a field operator he had experienced the darker and dangerous side of the business, now at forty–eight years old he was more useful as a Senior Intelligence Analyst. Borush returned to his cubicle and on his computer were the results of the search on Gfir.

It was very short and concise;

"No record of Subject, did not enter the country of Greece on any scheduled airline, ship, or crossed a border point."

Borush, then typed out another data search for all ships that arrived in Athens two weeks prior to the incident.

Within a half and hour he had a listing of all ships by name and owner. As he read the listing he saw the ship's name *MV Stellla Nova* that in it self did not trigger anything but the name of the owner did. He stopped for a minute to remember where he had heard this name before. Borush had earned his reputation as being a top operator because he used his memory to his advantage. His mind was like a steel trap, once he learned of anything it was stored. About a year ago, he and some other analysts were played a recording of a meeting between an Arab and a Dominican in Switzerland. The Arab was identified as one Osama bin Laden, and the Dominican as a Pedro Ordonez, primary owner of Consuelo Imports of Genoa. Now he knew how Gfir got into Athens. He passed his findings upstairs with a recommendation that Consuelo Imports should be a target of interest for the Mossad.

FIFTY-SIX

1988
Bass River Barracks

S TANSFIELD TOOK THE call.
"Dan, Tom Newcomb here, got some info for you."

"Hope it is good, go ahead Tom."

"Going to start with the *FV Sea Traveller* owned by Seaford Corporation. Operated by Captain Norman and Eileen Grayson, maiden name Blaine. Seaford Corporation within the past year, completed a one mile dredged channel above Tuckerton to a ship repair yard owned by DelMarVa Ship and Repair managed by an Anthony Conway. *MV Abigail Conway* and *MV Tiger star* reported missing at sea 1987. Lloyd's of London paid owner Seaford Corporation full claims. June 1985, a forty-two foot high-speed Huntress was impounded by Ocean City Maryland Police, it was found abandoned at a municipal dock. Police found traces of blood and cocaine. Listed owner of boat was Ralph Blaine, who claimed the boat was stolen a week before. Boat is still in impound."

Stansfield,

"Tom, great job. We may have identified some new evidence, call me anytime if you need anything."

"Will do Dan, and good luck."

As he ended the call, Newcomb saw a flashing message on his computer. It was coded, but Newcomb knew what it meant. His inquiries had triggered a software alert system that had detected a security break in the system. Answering the code with a password, Newcomb was able to bring up a telephone number on the base that coincided with the parameters of the Stansfield inquiry. He found a number listed as incoming as 609-445-2219 to a number on the base assigned to a Chief Petty Officer cubicle. Newcomb ran the 609 number on his system, and found it listed to the Seaford Corporation on Fire Road, Pleasantville, NJ. A further check showed calls from the CPO's office back to the Seaford number on different dates. He ran a check of the base directory and found the phone assigned to a Chief Petty Officer, Joshua Devens. Newcomb placed a call to Craig Boylan, Special Agent of the Coast Guard Criminal Investigation Service based in Washington, DC answered.

"Tom, how the hell are you, been a long time."

"Yes, it has been a long time since Da Nang. How's the family?

"Great, got 3 grandchildren, and enjoying every minute of it. What can I do for you Tom?

"Craig I got an information leak up here. The State Police are running an interstate triple homicide, and I have discovered phone calls coming and going out to a person of interest involved in this investigation. Got a name, just need you to catch him in the act."

"Give me the name."

"Chief Petty Officer Joshua Devens, stationed here and part of the OSE watch."

"I'll let you know when we pounce Tom."

"Thanks Craig."

CHAPTER FIFTY-SEVEN

1988
Long Neck, Delaware

R ED BLACKMAN WAS a great watcher and listener of people. When he had moved to South Jersey, he learned that the hustle and bustle of New York had to be left behind and a more quiet approach to the new surroundings. In Jack Nolan's Bar he was hardly noticed, because he looked like a seafarer. Ordering a beer, he sat quietly at the bar and looked and listened. There were about twenty people inside drinking and talking, some playing pool.

He motioned the bartender over and asked him if he knew of a good local repair dock for his boat. The bartender pointed him to two guys at the pool table. He went over to one of them an introduced himself,

"Hi, I'm Walt Jenkins. I just moved up here from

North Carolina, and my boat needs a repair. Bartender said maybe you can recommend a good local drydock."

One of the two looked at him, then looked at his friend and said,

"If it is a small job, go see old man Saunders. If it is a big job, head up to Toms River to Brady Marine."

"When I fueled up in Virginia, the guy recommended DelMarVa Ship and Repair, are they still in business?"

"Oh yeah, they're still in business but me and Eddy won't recommend them. Take your business to more honest people than Ralph Blaine."

"Hey thanks, let me buy you both a round, I sure appreciate it."

For the next two hours Blackman talked with his new found friends. Dickie Fosbury was the talker, and his buddy Mike Sarno chimed in when he had something to say. They both had worked for Ralph Blaine and had nothing good to say about him.

Sarno,

"You know Blaine lost his two sons. He fired us to bring them on."

"How did they die?"

Fosbury,

"They said lost at sea, but knowing them it was probably drugs."

Blackman,

"Did they ever find the bodies?"

"Well the funerals were pretty hushed up, only family attended. The only one I was sorry for was the mother, she wasn't like the rest of them."

"Lot of big fancy cars for those funerals, all out of state led by Ralph's sister's brother-in-law, the Chief of Police of Millsboro. That SOB would run me and Mike in for drinking, while the Blaine boys ran drugs, and he knew it" said Dickie.

Blackman,

"Well thanks guys for the help, I gotta get my ass up to Toms River."

They all shook hands and Red left the bar, eager to get back to Bass River.

FIFTY-EIGHT

1988
Manhattan North Homicide, NYPD

CHIEF INSPECTOR PHILIPPE Noire of Interpol took the call from New York.

"My dear friend Detective Feeney and how are you?"

"Good Phillipe, hope you and yours are safe and healthy."

"We are Sean, and what can I do for you."

"Did you get my e-mail request?"

"Yes, but we have very little information on this Seaford Corporation. They have surfaced in several drug smuggling incidents throughout Europe. Product came into country, but could not be found on board their ship. We boarded and searched the vessel and could not find anything, yet after a few days the product had been distributed."

"When was the last boarding?"

"February 12, 1986 in Marseille, the Seaford Corporation's *MV Tiger Star.*"

"Thank you my friend, my best to your family."

"Au revoir Sean"

Feeney's next call was to the FBI Headquarters in Washington, DC.

"Special Agent Czarowski please, NYPD Homicide calling."

After a few minutes,

"Sean, Checked on new offshore accounts for Seaford Corporation. Found new accounts in South Korea, China and the Philippines. We crosschecked the names Conway, Stoddard and Daniels found a notation in the Cayman Islands account. In 1978 Audra McClellan was removed from accounts custodian and replaced by a Danielle Thompson from that same Philadelphia law address. Further check on Audra McClellan had her presently living at 187 Skyline Drive, Feasterville, PA outside of Philly."

"Thanks Mikey, appreciate your help."

"Anytime Sean, take care."

# CHAPTER FIFTY- NINE

1988
Port of Barahona, Dominican Republic

M*V STELLA NOVA* arrived after a hectic Atlantic crossing of six days. Pedro Ordonez waited in his white Jaguar at the bottom of the gangway. Bin Laden had paid him a million dollars for the ship to ferry just one passenger.

As the unloading began as single white male dressed in a white linen suit walked down to the pier. Ordonez was only given a name. He left the cool insides of his car and approached the man.

"Mr. Malcolm McGuiness?"

"Yes, and you must be Mr. Ordonez, pleasure to meet you."

"Yes, now please get inside my air conditioned car, your suit will wrinkle out here. Your baggage will be brought to my house."

"Very good, I have heard good things about you and your company. The term discreet and efficient was used glowingly."

"Thank you for the compliment, we do try to impress our clients."

It took about twenty minutes to reach the palatial home of Ordonez, as they entered the long driveway heavily guarded by armed men. Servants came out and Ordonez and his guest went into the house.

"Miguel, please show Mr. McGuiness to the grand bedroom. Take a few hours to rest and freshen up, we will have dinner at 6PM."

"Thank you, you are gracious host."

Ordonez went into his private den. He remembered the communication from Bin Laden advising him that his emissary was important to his organization and he entrusted Ordonez with his safe passage into America. The million dollars would cover that very nicely. Ordonez was not interested in the workings of bin Laden, politically he was neutral. The money was good, and his alliance with the Saudi had made him millions in the new and expanding drug markets of Europe and the Middle East. As he sat there, his late brothers deaths came to mind, and his continuing war against Seaford needed to be continued. A year ago, he had enlisted a deep black company from Spain that provided him with information on Seaford. He went to his safe and pulled out a file marked, SEAFORD. Some 100 pages listed everything about the Conway's and their extended families. Names, locations, the type of operation, the bank accounts, the European and Asian business partners all neatly recorded in this single file. Ordonez and his two most trusted lieutenants had reviewed the file, actively looking for weak link. They found it amongst the casino client's payable accounts. The Excelsior, Hollywood, and Silver Nugget casinos owned by the Trap Organization was in arrears for some $100 million in equipment and services provided by the New Seaford Corporation. Known for its history of slow and non-payments, Trap was run by the bellicose Tommy Trap of New York. Trap had made his fame in New York real estate, and had joined the Atlantic City casino scene by opening the Excelsior. After the first year, Trap declared bankruptcy, re-organized and agreed to pay his creditors 25 cents on the dollar. Seaford took a loss but continued to do business with Trap. Then one day Tommy's father, the aging billionaire Gus Trap walked into the Casino. With four armed bodyguards carrying suitcases, he went to the first Bacarrat table he saw, laid out $50 million, and then stuffed the chips into the four suitcases and left the casino, never betting one chip. That was called a loan to sonny boy Tommy. The casino business took off and Trap opened two more casinos.

There were three good years of operation, then Trap divorced his first wife. The divorce became a scandal and she took a third of his empire. Once again the suppliers to Trap were owed money and New Seaford was one of the top three creditors. At this point in time Tommy Trap again declared bankruptcy, but this time went to the Russians and became their money launderer. Seaford got wind of the scheme, and had a head to head with Tommy. Andrew literally put a gun in Tommy's mouth and counted to three, Andrew became his silent partner. Seaford now laundered their ill-gotten gains through the Trap Organization. In the mind of Pedro Ordonez, the best way to create problems for the Conways was to take out Tommy Trap and pin it on New Seaford. He gave the go ahead for a plan to make it happen. Ordonez looked at his watch, and saw it was time for dinner and his overnight guest.

Ordonez,

"May I offer you a taste of my wine cellar, Mr. McGuiness?

"Please, I enjoy a hearty red."

Ordonez motioned to his butler and said,

"Alejandro, pick out a Merlot 1987 or a Burgundy 1981 for our guest."

The butler left the room. Ordonez sized up his guest. He was definitely Irish, well built and had large hands. His head was shaven, and it was obvious the man exercised regularly.

"Were you born in Ireland, Mr. McGuiness?"

"Northern Ireland, Belfast. Born and bred in the troubles."

Ordonez,

"I was in Belfast about a year ago, had business with a importer located on Styles Lane, very interesting man, he was a supplier to the Provisional IRA. I somehow forgot his name."

"His name was O'Connor and his business was on Skyles Lane."

"I take it your journey is for the IRA?"

"Mr. Ordonez, if it was, I couldn't tell you. Let's just say my present employer has me working on different jobs.

"Ah, here are a two of my marvelous reds from my cellar."

Alejandro poured the first one and offered it to the guest. He smelled the bouquet, then took a sip, swirled it around. As he swallowed he looked at Ordonez.

"A taste of pear with an oak accent, a true Burgundy."

Repeated the same with the other bottle he stated,

"Fragrances of lilac and spice a mighty Merlot, my compliments Mr. Ordonez your cellar is truly magnificent."

Ordonez nodded with a smile. The dinner was served and they both talked cordially till the end.

"We'll have some brandy on the terrace."

As they overlooked the nighttime harbor, McGuiness spoke first.

"I believe I will be leaving tomorrow, can you tell me the arrangements."

"The Consuelo freighter, *Lorcon D'Or* will be leaving Barahona for stops in the United States. You will be given a Barbados passport as a member of the crew. Your first stop will be Charleston, South Carolina, after unload, you will pass customs, and at a portside restaurant you will be picked up and taken to a safe house in Charleston. New identity will be issued and you will fly to Newark, New Jersey. I was told you have taken care of the arrangements from that point, am I correct?"

"Yes, everything has been set up to begin our operation."

"Well, Mr. McGuiness, the best of luck to you and your employer."

They lifted their glasses of brandy and nodded.

CHAPTER SIXTY

1988
Feasterville, Pennsylvania

187 SKYLINE DRIVE was a two-story craftsman type home. Flowers bristled the walkway, and a sign read, "at Grammy's house there are no rules, just hugs, kisses and cookies". Sean Feeney rang the bell twice. Soon the door opened, answered by an older woman wearing an apron.

"Can I help you?" she asked.

Sean showed her his badge and credentials.

"Are you Audra McClellan?"

"Yes."

"Ms. McClellan I need to talk to you about your employment at Conway, Stoddard and Daniels. My investigation entails the murders of Vincent Conway Jr., Patrick and Timothy Blaine, can we talk?"

The woman hesitated at first, then said,

"Please come in."

Feeney entered a well kept and clean living room, she motioned him to a chair.

"Can I offer you some coffee or tea?"

"Coffee, black would be fine."

As he sat in the chair, he noticed a wedding picture, several small photos of children spaced on the wall and side tables. She re-entered with a steaming cup of coffee. Sitting across from Feeney, she took a deep breath and said,

"I worked over 35 years for that firm. They were very nice to me, and my family, but I knew the day would come when the police would show up. I will try and answer your questions as best I can."

"That is all I ask. Now did you know Vincent Conway Jr.?"

"Yes, from when he was a baby to when he died."

"What was he like?"

"A spoiled brat with a silver spoon. I never liked him, he was always getting into trouble, and his father always was bailing him out. He cost the firm a lot of money. I was in charge of firm real property, and Vinny Jr. must have wrecked about four company cars. The rent on his New York apartment was over the top, but Conway Sr. felt it was best to placate him. His brother Mark was a gentleman and much smarter than Vinny, he never got the attention his brother got. I know it is not right to say ill of the dead, but you just knew he would end up that way."

"Did you know he had a drug problem?"

"No, no one ever mentioned it."

"Did you know the Blaine brothers?"

"No, not personally, but I knew the father Ralph. The firm represented his business, DelMarVa Ship."

"Were there any problems with that relationship?"

"Can't remember anything outside the course of normal business."

"You were listed as a custodian for the firm bank account in the Cayman Islands. Was there a reason you were removed?"

"Well one day I was told to wire a large amount of money to a account that I knew was not a client, so I went to Conway Sr. to verify. He told me wait, while he made a call. He called Andrew Conway at Seaford International. I heard him ask to whom the money was for, and he just nodded and hung up. He then told me it was money held in escrow, and it was alright for me to proceed with the transfer. I got back to my desk, and before I gave approval for the transfer. I checked on the recipient. I made sure I noted the date and time, the receiving bank and the recipients name, then approved the transfer."

"How much was the wire for?"

"$100 million."

"Who was the recipient?"

"Tommy Trap, Chase Manhattan Bank, New York, Kips Bay Branch."

"Where there ever any other transfers like that again?"

"The next month to the date another $100 million, then again the following month for $85 million."

"All this money came from what account?"

"Seaford International, Andrew Conway CEO."

"Why were you replaced as account custodian?"

"I was never told the reason why, just turn it over to Danielle Thompson. I did and the next month they offered me a very nice retirement package."

"Is Danielle Thompson a relative of Conway Sr.?"

"Her mother is his first cousin. Danielle is an attorney, graduated Stanford Law and is a very nice person."

"Had you ever met, Andrew Conway?"

"No, not in my time there."

"Did Tommy Trap ever come to the office?"

"No, never saw him either."

"Well, thank you for your time, you have been a great help. If I have to talk to you again, can I call you here?

"Call anytime Detective, I'm not going anywhere."

CHAPTER SIXTY-ONE

1988
NJ State Police Station, Bass River

A SKILLED INVESTIGATOR GIVEN the facts must then sort out the chaff from the wheat. Dan Stansfield, knew he had to verify the clues from the abandoned Huntress in Ocean City, Maryland. He had asked the Ocean City Police to test the blood evidence and cocaine residue that was found on the boat. After a few weeks he was now in possession of the lab results. He could compare it to the blood evidence from both Blaine brother's scenes. As he opened the envelope he quickly scanned it to the second page. He smiled. The blood found on the boat was from 2 different persons. One was A positive, the other A negative. Patrick Blaine was A positive, and Timothy was A negative. Next he looked at the

DNA markers from the boat evidence, the haplotype numbers were conclusive. Both Blaine brothers were on the high speed Huntress when they were shot. Stansfield could only surmise, Patrick must have died instantly from his head wound, then dumped overboard. Timothy was stomach shot then airlifted away. Why he was dropped over the Dorothy manufacturing plant? Stansfield chalked that up as a non-planned unscheduled incident. Timothy was to be buried in the Pine Barrens never to be found. The father Ralph Blaine had lied, Patrick had come back to the family. As to what the brothers were doing on the boat together, the cocaine residue found on the boat was compared to the cocaine residue found in the lungs of Patrick, and the shirt of Timothy. These all matched. Stansfield had Red Blackman's visit to Long Neck, Delaware and the statements that the brothers were smuggling in drugs. A high-speed 42 foot ocean boat could range out into the ocean some 200 miles, meet another ship, and load some tonnage of cocaine, then come back to DelMarVa Ship and Tool before dawn. The brothers were intercepted at sea, one was killed, the other was wounded and airlifted. The boat with its valuable cargo hijacked was abandoned. The motive was to hurt the Seaford operation. Olsen's report on Consuelo Imports certainly matched the reasoning.

The Ordonez vendetta for the Brown place massacre only meant more was going to happen. It was now a matter of time before Pedro Ordonez acted.

CHAPTER SIXTY-TWO

1988
Tangier, Morocco

T HE HOTEL CHELLAH was a very tired place that was in need of a refurbishment. For the needs of Hector, it was sufficient. Not a place to warrant any attention, the meeting with Andrew Conway would be private and secure. Hector had rented two connecting rooms, and left word at the desk that his business associate a Mr. Harold McGill of Toronto would be checking in a noon.

At 1PM Hector opened the adjoining room door and shook hands with Andrew Conway. As both men sat done Hector offered his guest a glass of Red Breast Irish Whiskey. Andrew smiled, and offered a toast to their continued relationship.

Hector,

"I have found and tracked your two ships. The *Abigail Conway* is now known at the *Trade Fortune*, while your older ship the *Tiger Star* is now the *Stella Nova*. The *Abigail* was hijacked at sea by Al Queda, you remember the Saudi Osama bin Laden. The *Tiger Star* was handed over by her captain, the Filipino named Braco. Both ships were modified in appearance and have since been plying the Mediterranean routes from Africa to Europe. My people have followed them and taken videos. In Genoa we watched the *Trade Fortune* unload its regular cargo, then in the early hours of the next morning we observed a hold opening and four people exit the ship.

Later a briefcase was delivered to the Captain. We watched as he left the ship and followed. He went into a building, entered into a business, then left without the briefcase. In Yanbu, Saudi Arabia we watched the *Stella Nova* load up with cargo, then 20 persons got on the ship. Following her to Athens we watched the 20 people leave the ship after the unload. We got good videos. The next day was the *City of Poros* terrorist bombing and attack. We were able to match the face of one of the terrorists, with a photo of him leaving the Stella Nova. He was a Palestinian trained by Al Queda. Your ships are now being used to transport Al Queda terrorists to the European continent. I mentioned we tracked the Captain of the *Trade Fortune* to a business in Genoa. That business is Consuelo Imports, also listed as the owners of both ships. Consuelo has two offices, the one in Genoa and the main office in Barahona, Dominican Republic".

Conway,

"So, I am a victim of Osama bin Laden. You know I refused his offer to do business. Hector, who is this Consuelo Imports?"

"Very little, I am sorry to say, but we have the name of the CEO, a Pedro Ordonez"

Conway, reacted as if a gun had gone off.

"That was the name of the drug dealers in the Bronx that we wiped out. Son of a bitch, we must have missed this guy. Now it all comes together, Pedro Ordonez is out for revenge, so he teamed up with bin Laden and has caused me some grief."

"Andrew, what do want me to do?"

"First, track down Bracos and kill him. When that is done we will decide what to do with Ordonez."

"Very well, I will notify you when we have finished the job."

CHAPTER SIXTY-THREE

1989
Mossad, Tel Aviv

IT WAS JANUARY 25th, 15 days after the Pan Am Flight 103 bombing over Lockerbie, Scotland. The name Abdelbasset Meghrahi put all the intelligence agencies focus on Libya. Muammar Gadaffi was the main person of interest, for there were connections between Meghrahi and Gadaffi's secret service, the Mukhabarat el-Jemahiriya. Was the bombing orchestrated by Gadaffi? If you had polled the world intelligence agencies, 99% would have pinned the blame on Gadaffi, but Tal Borush was the 1% that knew the real truth. When he infiltrated Libya in 1981, he had met Meghrahi, who at the time was a college student intent on overthrowing the Gaddaffi regime. Borush's report back to Mossad simply stated that:

"Though Meghrahi talked the talk, he was not fully committed to regime overthrow. There seemed to be an underlying dedication for action by radical Islam terrorism."

Borush had continued to keep tabs on Meghrahi connections and movements. In 1987 Meghrahi arrived in Cyprus, then took a flight to Yemen. He was gone for six weeks, then he was seen again in Cyprus boarding a plane for Libya. Just like Gfir, he had physically changed, more muscular and a definite weight loss. Meghrahi had attended the Al Queda training camp, and the result was the Pan Am Flight 103 bombing. Gadaffi was the obvious madman and scapegoat, but Borush knew who planned the bombing. Osama bin Laden was the mastermind, while his cohort Pedro Ordonez was the transporter. He wrote up his findings, and passed it up to the director. In this business he had cultivated "friends" whom he had coordinated with through the years, in this case he felt he would make it known to a close American friend working with the FBI. It had been about a year since they last spoke. They had met in New York City when a suspected IRA bomb maker had eluded the British MI-5 the suspect entered the US with a Canadian passport. Borush knew where he would find refuge, because there was some fervent support amongst the Irish-American community. He met this FBI agent at PJ Clarks bar in Manhattan. Borush told the agent he would be wearing a Tottenham Hot Spurs sweat shirt, the agent would be wearing a Mets baseball cap. They spotted each other, sat down and drank for the next 4 hours. They hit it off as if they were friends from long ago. Borush gave his new friend an address in, Rockaway, NY where the fugitive would be hiding. The FBI stormed the house and arrested the IRA bomber. The agent in one arrest had made himself a name in the Bureau, as well as cementing any frayed relations with British MI-5. He was indebted to Borush, and their friendship flourished. Borush picked up the phone and called Washington, DC.

The agent picked up his phone,

"Mike Czarowski"

"You still wearing that Mets hat?"

"Tal, good to here from you. You know that was my spy hat, I'm really a Yankees fan.

They both laughed.

"Mike, I may have something for you. Are you on a secure line?"

"Yes, go ahead."

"Where is the FBI in regard to the Pan Am bombing?"

"Everyone is concentrated on Gadaffi. He is getting all the attention, why do you ask?"

"I believe the real fox got away and your chasing a false trail."

"You mean Meghrahi is not the culprit?"

"Mike, he is the culprit, but his master is not Gadaffi, it is a new name, a very fast rising star with a new message and following."

"Who?"

"A Saudi by the name of Osama bin Laden. He's rich, he's connected, he has support, and he has the ear of the downtrodden."

"Tal, that name has never come up in my circles, how did you get onto him?"

"We were watching these training camps spring up in Yemen. Recruits from all over: PLO, IRA, Bader-Meinhof, Muslim Brotherhood, and Chechen Militia. We interrogated a "graduate", and he gave us bin Laden.

About a year ago we latched onto bin Laden meeting someone in Switzerland, got a recording of that meeting and we have been following both. The *City of Poros* attack was done by a Palestinian named Gfir. He went to the camp in Yemen. He was smuggled into Athens by a boat owned by the guy who met bin Laden in Switzerland. I believe Meghrahi was Yemen trained, and he also got into Athens via that same boat."

"Who is this boat owner?"

"We identified him as owner and CEO of a company called Consuelo Imports, name is Pedro Ordonez.

"Tal, this is a longshot because everybody is focused on crazy Gadaffi. This is the first I ever heard of this guy bin Laden, he is not anyone's radar screen, except yours.

This Ordonez is another out in left field name, what do you want me do? If I stray away from the Gadaffi track, my bosses will send me to Montana and I will be staking out cattle rustlers.

"Mike I understand the situation, but just keep this close to the vest. Maybe feel out from your sources and contacts if they know or heard anything. If something comes back, get back to me."

"Ok, it is inside my right vest pocket, if anything pops up, you get the call."

"Thanks Mike, thanks for listening to me."

"Tal, Shalom."

"And Shalom to you."

# CHAPTER SIXTY-FOUR

1989
Cape May Coast Guard Base

H E TOOK THE call at 2pm.
"Josh, need you to give me anything on two boats. One is called the *Trade Fortune* and the other the *Stella Nova*. *Check out* a company called Consuelo Imports, Dominican Republic."

Chief Devens replied,

"Should take me a day, I'll be back to you.

The call ended, and as Coast Guard Chief Devens got back to the paperwork on his desk, he failed to see the two non-uniformed men enter his office area. His attention was focused on his desk when a hand and holding a badge appeared. He looked up.

"Joshua Devens, you are under arrest for passing

classified information. Stand up and put your arms behind you."

About 3 hours later Special Agent Craig Boylan made a call to Tom Newcomb.

"He folded and gave us Andrew Conway at New Seaford. It appears they are related. Devens mother maiden name was Thompson, a second cousin to Conway."

"Thanks Craig, I owe you one."

Newcomb placed a call to Dan Stansfield.

"Dan, we found our leak here, and he will be gone for awhile. Just want to tell you that this guy's mother was a second cousin to Andrew Conway, from the Thompson side."

'Well that explains a lot, thanks Tom, great work."

CHAPTER SIXTY-FIVE

1989
Excelsior Casino Parking Garage
Atlantic City, NJ

IT WAS A very fast operation with clock like military precision. As Tommy Trap left his penthouse apartments, he was escorted to the top deck of the garage where his Rolls Royce Corniche awaited him for a trip to Philadelphia. In the first several seconds his bodyguards were put down. Trap was injected in the neck, and was placed inside a black van by two masked men. Within 20 seconds it was all over Tommy Trap was kidnapped in broad daylight. The black van was found in nearby Pleasantville abandoned. As Police were alerted, and roadblocks set up, there were no demands for the next three days.

Meanwhile in the DelMarVa Repair yard north of

Tuckerton, Anthony Conway caught the movement of ship coming up the channel. Anthony expected this ship some 6 hours earlier after he had a phone conversation with the Captain. The ship *Carib Palm*, 75 meters long and 887 tons was in need of an electric repair in the engine room. The owners in Belgium had wired some $100 thousand dollars toward the eventual cost of the repair. Anthony had turned a profit for Seaford by doing legitimate business, as well as servicing the replacement secret hold ships. As the *Carib Palm* maneuvered towards the dock, ropes were thrown and the ship was tied to the dock. Captain Guillermo Negras, master of the *Carib* departed the ship to meet with Anthony Conway in his office. In turn teams of DelMarVa workers boarded the ship to begin the needed repairs. In his office Anthony and Captain discussed the time the repair would take, and for the Captain and his crew to prepare for a three day stoppage. The Captain understood and advised Conway he and his crew would try and stay away from the work area. Anthony also advised him that U.S. Customs prohibited him and his crew from leaving the property of the shipyard. Negras assured him they would remain aboard the ship. The repairs commenced and for the next 2 days the engine room was a scene of noise and light. On the morning of the third day after midnight someone came down the gangway, and using lock picks entered Conway's office. At his desk they opened drawers, by the third one they found a Taurus 9mm pistol. Wearing plastic gloves they took the gun and left the office. Another unknown figure from the ship opened the front gates to let in a blue Ford Taurus bearing NJ plates. Both inside operatives got in a car and drove down a road that surrounded the repair yard. About a half mile from the shipyard, the car stopped and all three people got out. They opened the trunk and removed three shovels. They started digging near a chain link fence. When finished they had dug a shallow hole about three feet deep. Then all three went back to the trunk. One of them turned on a flashlight while the other two unwrapped the large sheet wrapped package. Tommy Trap was alive his arms and feet tied, and his mouth gagged. The flash-light was directed at his face, and he could not see his captors. The 9mm came out and a makeshift suppres-sor was attached in the form of a one liter plastic soda bottle. The first shot hit his heart, blood splattered the shooter, but death was instantaneous. The next two shots were thru both eyes. The bound body was taken to the grave and covered. The three assassins got back in the car drove back to the gate, two got out of the car. One opened the gate and the car drove away from the shipyard. The gate was relocked, and that figure got back on the ship.

The remaining figure using the lock picks got back into the office and placed the pistol back in the correct drawer. Leaving he re-locked the office and made his way up the gangway onto the *Carib Palm* That morning all repairs were finished and the ship pulled out for its next port Bermuda. Anthony sat down for his morning coffee and read the headlines in the local paper. Tommy Trap's disappearance was the main news, with no new leads. Anthony thought about his father and his dealings with Trap. Without Trap to launder Seaford's money, could there be a problem?

Then he noticed two New Jersey State Police cruisers enter the shipyard. The troopers exited their vehicles and entered his office.

"Good morning how can I help you?"

"Are you Anthony Conway?"

"Yes, I am."

"This is a search warrant for these premises and property."

He handed the paper to Anthony, the other trooper spoke into his radio and said,

"The warrant has been served, come on in."

In the course of the next two minutes some fifteen police cars entered the property. Two plain clothes men wearing FBI raid jackets entered the office and told Anthony to remove himself from the building, while they executed the warrant. Anthony left and got inside his car. He placed a call to his father. The police and FBI separated into teams and for the next two hours examined everything. They found a 9mm pistol in the drawer and placed it in a plastic evidence bag. Then there was chatter on the radios. A police K-9 unit had uncovered something down the shipyard road. A body was unearthed. A medical examiner was present. His examination stated that person had died within the past 10 hours, and it appeared the weapon used was a 9mm.

Further search of the burial site found three spent 9mm shells. The FBI agents asked Anthony if the pistol in his office drawer belonged to him.

"Yes, and I have a permit showing it belongs to me."

His arms were taken placed behind him and he was handcuffed.

"Anthony Conway you are under arrest for the murder of Thomas Trap, you have the right to remain silent, you have the right to an attorney, if you cannot afford an attorney one will be provided for you. Do you understand what I have just told you?"

In total disbelief Anthony said,

"Yes. I will remain silent and wish to call my attorney."

At Seaford International offices Andrew was on the phone to Vincent Conway in Philadelphia.

"Vincent, the police had a warrant to search my

shipyard in Tuckerton, now I just learned they found the body of Tommy Trap and arrested my son for his murder. My son is being framed.

"Andrew, I'll have him represented at the arraignment as soon as we find out where they are holding him."

"Thank you Vincent."

In Barahona, Pedro Ordonez received a call telling him that the plan worked and Conway's son was arrested.

He smiled as he hung up the phone.

# CHAPTER SIXTY-SIX

1989
New York City

MALCOLM MCGUINESS WAS now known as Freddy Donnely. When he reached Manhattan, he reached out for assistance and called a phone number he was given.

The wealthy Irish-American contractor and loyal IRA supporter Ray McBride was expecting the call. McBride headed the organization called the Friends of Armagh, the source of American money for the IRA. He had been instructed by his sources in Belfast to provide whatever assistance the caller wanted. This person was very important to the IRA, and must be hidden in full view.

He needed to be employed as an engineer, and would construct a device for the Friends of Armagh.

McBride had volunteered to set off a device on American soil against a British target.

McBride,

"Can you meet me in 2 hours?"

"Sure, give me the address."

"The Old Public House, 88th Street and Fort Hamilton Parkway, Bay Ridge, Brooklyn. I'll be wearing a blue jacket and yellow shirt."

"Fine, I will see you in 2 hours."

They met as planned, and to anybody looking on, it was like two friends meeting. By the 2nd pint of Guinness, Freddy had outlined his needs and McBride stated everything would be in order by the next day. McBride wrote down an address and told him it was a safe place to spend the night. He gave Freddie $1500 in cash, and said.

"My car will pick you up tomorrow morning at 8AM and bring you to my office, everything will be ready."

Leaving the bar, he took a taxi to the address. It was a single house off of Ocean Parkway. A lady came to the door. Freddy introduced himself and told her Mr. McBride had sent him. She said her name was Colleen Murphy and she would show him his room. Taking him upstairs to a single bedroom, he was shown where the bathroom was, and if he was hungry to come down to the kitchen and she would prepare something. He was hungry so he followed her to the kitchen. In talking to Colleen he learned she was born in Northern Ireland and she despised the British. She had lost her two brothers, and a fiancée to British Army bullets. She had come to America some ten years ago and had married a man named Murphy. He was a tugboat Captain and they had purchased this house. Two years into the marriage there was a collision, and he was killed. He had left her a lot of money and the house. She helped Mr. McBride and the cause by providing food and shelter for "special visitors.

"I guess I'm a special visitor. Can I ask you something Mrs. Murphy?"

"Yes." she replied.

"Would you rent me that room by the week?"

"I guess I could.

They agreed to a price over coffee. He thanked her for the food and talk and went up to his room. The next morning McBride's car was outside. He was taken to commercial area and entered a six-story office building. The elevator took him to the top floor of McBride Construction and Development. He was escorted to the owner's office and offered a seat. McBride came in shook his hand, and placed a large envelope on the table.

"This is everything you requested. Where will you be staying?"

"I've decided to rent a room from Mrs. Murphy."

"Good idea. Did you ever play football?"

"Yes, sometime ago."

"Do not call me, I will not bother you at your rooming house, but if we need to meet it will be on Saturday mornings at Ketchum Park. You should join the Irish League that plays there, they always need players, and it is a good idea for all newcomers to be accepted into the community."

"Sounds good Mr. McBride and thank you for everything."

They shook hands and he left. Returning to his room, he closed the door and opened the envelope. There was a New York State drivers license, a US passport, and a Social Security card all in the name of one Brian Patrick Tynan. Next he was directed to report to a Mr. Hal Lynch at the Metro Maintenance Corporation, 30 Broadway, Manhattan where he would be given a job. A diploma in the name of Bryan Tynan from Cardinal Spellman High School, and a Bachelor's Degree in Air Conditioning Technology from Stryer University dated 1987. He opened another envelope that contained a Walther 9mm and 2 extra clips and a stack of money totaling $20,000. Now his assignment in New York would begin with everything he needed. He thought about how long he had been at this work, and his mind wandered back to his parents in Northern Ireland. The son of hard working Catholics: Sheila and Robert Callahan, he had experienced the troubles first hand. During his teens he never was interested in the cause, but kept his mind on mathematics and science. It turned out for the good, for he was a most gifted student. He received a full scholarship to the Imperial College in London. Four year later he held a degree in Mechanical Engineering with honors. He accepted a job in London with a prestigious engineering firm, and was given important projects, all at which he excelled. Then on November of 1978 his uncle called to tell him that his parents were killed in a pub bombing. The Ulster Volunteer Army claimed responsibility. Returning for the burials, he sought out his cousin Tim Riordan. Tim was IRA, and he had decided he would fight the British and the Protestants to the death. Martin Callahan was welcomed in, and it was there that he became a master bomb maker. Using his engineering expertise he wrought havoc on both the British Army and the Ulster Protestants. A price was soon on his head and he had to leave Northern Ireland. His reputation got him noticed by one Osama bin Laden who convinced him to hone his skills working for Al Queda. He left for the training camps in Yemen. There he trained hundreds and developed more lethal bombs.

Now sitting in Brooklyn he would meet the next day with Hal Lynch who would assign his new Heating Ventilation and Cooling expert to his biggest client, the New York World Trade Center.

CHAPTER SIXTY-SEVEN

1989
NJ State Police Station - Bass River

A S AGREED ALL the parties met for their monthly
get together. Stansfield seated at the head of the
table started the meeting off.

"Since our last time together we have established
that both Blaine brothers were on the reported missing 42 foot Huntress. Blood and drug evidence has
supported that Patrick Blaine was killed on board,
and most likely dumped overboard. Timothy Blaine
was shot in the stomach on board, but airlifted via a
helicopter for burial on land. The burial area was pre-
sumed to be the Pine Barrens, but something happened
causing Timothy Blaine to fall from the aircraft onto
the Attentive Pharmaceutical property in Dorothy,
where his fall was fatal. The evidence of cocaine found

on both victims matched with traces found on the boat deck. It would be safe to say the Huntress was transporting cocaine from a mother ship located outside our international boundary. The Huntress was then stopped at sea by a helicopter and boarded. The cargo was taken somewhere, and the boat abandoned in Ocean City, Maryland. We now can say with what we know of the New Seaford Corporation and their family network that this was an on going smuggling operation for Seaford. The perpetrators of this hijacking and murder are slowly pointing to relationships to the family Ordonez massacre of Brown Place and its heirs presently situated in the Dominican Republic. Sean interviewed a Audra McCellan, a former employee of Conway, Stoddard and Daniels. She was the custodian of the firms' Cayman Islands account. During her stewardship there were three very large transfers from the firm's escrow account to the late Tommy Trap. We believe this was money to be laundered for New Seaford. As you all know, Tommy Trap was kidnapped and murdered. It appears Anthony Conway son of Andrew has been arrested and charged in this case. In my opinion how convenient in a series of attacks upon New Seaford by the Dominican Republic based Ordonez family. A smaller item is that a source of ours, the Coast Guard OSE recently found a leak and caught the perp who was giving maritime intelligence information to New Seaford, turns out to be a distant relationship to the Conways. The CGCIS will not pursue any charges against New Seaford until our case is resolved. They will hold the leaker incommunicado under UMJ rules. Alright does anyone else have anything to add?

Sean Feeney signaled he had something. Stansfield acknowledged him.

"This has nothing to do with this case, but a mutual friend of this group Mike Czarnowski, FBI, Washington gave me a heads up on a international terrorist alert. The FBI has reason to believe there may be a terrorist action against the United States. If any of you come across the name Osama bin Laden, give Mike a call, it is important."

Sharon Olsen,

"I'll get what I can on this bin Laden"

"Thanks Sharon."

Red Blackman,

"That arrest for the Trap murder happened at the DelMarVA ship repair yard a little north of Tuckerton. Dan can your Coast Guard friend give us any info on the yard activity of that site? That narrow passage channel requires Coast Guard notification before entry."

"Will do Red."

As each team member got up to leave, no one said

it, but this case was an endless circle with no break. Murders had been committed, the perpetrators either a Conway or Ordonez, yet where was the solid evidence to break the case? What they needed was a small seam to open that would expand, then, they would have their evidence. They all knew from experience that when a investigation stalled or seemed endless, the break would come. That seam was now beginning to unravel in Tel Aviv.

SIXTY-EIGHT

1989
Tel Aviv

T HEY WERE ONCE enemies, now friends. That described the relationship between Tal Borush and Miro Fomani. Fomani once had Borush trapped and surrounded in Cairo, but he got away. Fomani now a under secretary of Egyptian Intelligence, the Mukhabarat sent a encrypted email to Borush's home computer that they had to meet. Borush responded and they decided to meet in Elat, Israel's Red Sea resort. Borush had great respect for Fomani, since the Peace treaty in 1979 he and Tal had worked together both trying to keep a lid on the powder keg known as the Middle East. Information was key to their success, for both their countries were the targets of the jihad terrorist. Borush remembered back to the fall of Lebanon, when Syria and its minions created the deadly civil war that tore apart a once vibrant country. Beirut was then known as the Zurich of the Middle East. There a consortium of Muslim and Christian business minds ran the country. This was where the power deals were made with the rest of the world, and the Middle East states profited. Whenever a prophet of Jihad arose they were given money and told to go away. Syria invaded and with its Hezbolah, Hamas and PLO allies the Christian influence was overthrown and destroyed. The power vacuum was moved to Riyadh, Saudi Arabia and the Royal court. The Saudi Royal Court was more hated by the Muslim Jihadists than the Israelis. There was no money to be made. The jihadist culture expanded and more terrorist incidents began all over the world. Osama bin Laden took his place in line with the other players, causing both Egypt and Israel to co-operate together on all terrorist intelligence matters. Borush was seated in the bar of the 4-star hotel, when he saw Fomani enter. They hugged and gave the traditional Arab greeting, then began their conversation.

Fomani,

"Tal my friend, you look well for an old washed out spy, what is your recipe for looking so spry."

"They wanted to promote me to Under Secretary, and I said no."

They both laughed.

Borush,

"And you Miro, the family is fine?"

"I'm a grandfather again, my son had a boy, all is well."

"Mazel Tov."

"Thank you my friend."

They continue to small talk for the next ten minutes, when Fomani broached his reason for the meeting.

"Al Queda's bomb maker is on the move. We had him in Yemen, but he got away. Then we got lucky, a source in Yanbu saw him get on a ship, and leave. What was odd, he walked up the gangway, and nothing else was loaded onto the ship, just him."

"Do you know the where the ship's next port of call?"

"Genoa, but it never arrived."

"What was the name of the ship?"

"The *MV Stella Nova*, out of Genoa owned….."

Borush interrupted,

"By Consuelo Imports."

"How did you know that?"

"Consuelo transports all of bin Laden's operatives. They have a deal. Tell me you have a photo of this person?"

"We got one shot, very grainy, but we estimate him to be about 187 centimeters, 84 kilo. He is Caucasian, and is right handed. We bribed the customs agent who said his name was Malcolm McGregor of Dublin, Ireland."

Borush thought for a minute, then looked at his friend.

"bin Laden is going to mount an operation that is big, something with a big bang that everyone will hear. I suggest you get your people working up some counter measures and try and locate this subject."

"I trust your evaluation. I will be in touch my friend."

"Thank you so much, I will be making my calls and hope somebody latches onto this operator."

They shook hands and both departed the bar. Tal was on the phone while on the plane back to Tel Aviv. He had alerted British MI-6, French DGSI, and the Canadian CSIS. He placed separate calls to America. At the CIA, he knew an assistant director and gave him the update. Next he called Mike Czarnowski.

"Mike, this is Tal. We suspect that Al Queda may be planning something, and it may be in your country. Remember that company Consuelo Imports, well I believe they may have brought over a master bomb maker. He is one of the best, and he has been in Yemen as the chief bomb maker and instructor. All we have is a very grainy photo and some stats. Our lab here is trying to get more out of the photo, I'll let you know if anything comes up."

"Ok, Tal we'll get it out. On what you told me the last time we spoke regarding this bin Laden, some of the views are changing here. Some have heard of him and are taking notices, his name is slowly coming up and entering conversations, so thank you."

"That is good to hear, maybe he can been given priority on the next to assassinate list, he's number one on ours."

"If anything happens you will hear from me. Take care Tal."

"Shalom to you Mike.

CHAPTER SIXTY-NINE

Singapore
1989

MANUAL RUIZ WAS a successful businessman in Singapore. He resided in the far north part of Singapore called the Woodlands. His wealth came from his ownership of some 85 franchises. From Kentucky Fried Chicken, McDonalds, and Chick-fil-A he was worth millions. Few knew about the man for he was very understated and private. No immense wealthy mansion, no expensive cars, no trophy wife. He was just a smart rich guy who drove a Ford pickup, and worked his businesses. Outwardly, his only extravagance was his 75-foot sailboat and his membership at the Republic of Singapore Yacht Club. Deemed an excellent sailor, he was the defending champion of the club's regatta. His home was large, modest, and off the beaten path. One thing for certain was that Manual Ruiz never called attention to himself for his wealth was never on display.

The Johor Causeway was only a few minutes from his home. His millions were stored in the vaults of the OCBC Bank in Johor, Malaysia, and his desire to always have access to his money was very important. His arrival in Singapore some two years ago was hardly noticed. He had visited previously and had invested in his first franchise, a McDonalds. His brother and sister managed it while he worked around the world. It was only in the last two years that he had moved to Singapore. As he prepared to go into the center of Singapore city he never noticed the dark blue Mercedes following his pickup. For the next half hour he was followed. As he parked his pickup in an underground garage, two men exited the Mercedes and approached him from the back. He did not see him, but stopped in his tracks when one called out to him.

"Arturo Bracos we have a message for you from the New Seaford Corporation."

Conway had found him, as he turned around, the two men had their pistols aimed at him. The first shot hit him dead center between his eyes. He dropped like a rock, his last thought was his gold in the bank vault.

The gunman got back in the Mercedes and left for their hotel. In a few minutes their employer picked up his phone in Sardinia. Paolo Sassari smiled, and told his crew to stay in Singapore for the next three days, then fly back to Italy. Paolo made a call to the United States.

Andrew Conway picked up and received the very good news from Hector. Still smiling he advised Hector to proceed with a surveillance of Pedro Ordonez.

CHAPTER SEVENTY

1989
FBI, Washington, DC

CZARNOWSKI TOOK THE call from Israel. Tal told him they had identified the man in the photo, and British MI6 verified it. Martin Callahan was the bomb maker's name, a highly wanted IRA fugitive. He was a mechanical engineer and had fled Ireland many years ago. With this, Czarnowski alerted his contacts. When he called Feeney, he was told to leave a message, which he would not do. Feeney had given him Blackman's number some time ago in case he could not get in touch with him. Blackman picked up his phone and called. Blackman answered,

"Hello"

"Red, Mike Czarnowski, how are you?

"Long time Mikey, Sean told me he was in contact with you, what's up."

"Did Sean ever brief you on a terrorists alert involving a subject by the name of bin Laden?"

"Yes, he did at our last meeting."

"Ok, I have some new info, so write this down."

"I don't write, just talk, my mind is like a safe" Czarnowski laughed.

"There is a bin Laden master bomb maker who was brought to the U.S. His real name is Martin Callahan, a IRA fugitive. Have no location for him as of present. If you get a smell of this guy let me know asap."

"How did he get into the country?"

"By a shipping company that bin Laden uses."

"Got a name?"

"Consuelo Imports out of the Dominican Republic."

"Did you just say Consuelo Imports?"

"Yes Red,"

"Consuelo imports out of the Dominican Republic run by Pedro Ordonez?"

"How the hell did you know that Red?"

"The triple homicide case we are working here involves two warring companies, New Seaford and a Consuelo Imports. Looks like we have the same interests Mikey."

"Red, get in touch with Sean and let him know.

I will be talking to the bosses here, and getting your group up to date."

"Will do."

"Good to be working with you again Bagels."

"And you also Mikey."

CHAPTER SEVENTY-ONE

1989
Briarcliff Manor, NY

SHARON OLSEN BEGAN the Osama bin Laden inquiry. With the following background information garnered from international news agencies, financial institutions, and foreign government releases she was able to develop a picture of this "unknown man." Born into wealth, he inherited some twenty-five to thirty million dollars after the death of his father the construction magnate of Saudi Arabia. He fought the Russians in Afghanistan, sometimes using his own money to purchase weapons. When the Russians pulled out of Afghanistan he returned to Saudi Arabia with his own legion of troops. These troops would provide the basis for the Sunni influenced Al Queda. He left Saudi Arabia after the Royal House of Saud invited America

troops to be stationed in northern Saudi Arabia against
the intrusion of Iraq's Saddam Hussein. With loyal
friends in Yemen he set up training camps to spread
his form of terrorism. These training camps trained
the Palestine Liberation Organization, Hezbollah,
Hamas, parts of the Muslim Brotherhood, the IRA,
Bader-Meinhof, Chechnya rebels, and the Japanese
Red Army group. Here a client's student would receive
military training in infantry tactics, sabotage, terrorism, bomb making, intelligence gathering and weapons expertise. Al Queda's enemies were the United
States, Saudi Arabia, Egypt, and Western European
nations, Shia Muslims and Israel. All operations were
geared toward their destruction.

Olsen then placed all this information into the
Holly-Lane 8 program and came up with some new
information. A large amount of bank activity, namely
transfers of monies from the accounts of The Saudi
Arabian Foreign Auto Board based in northern city of
Ar'ar to the Central Saudi Construction Partnership
in Khobar. These transfers in the past five years totaled
some four hundred million dollars. The sole owner of
the Foreign Car Board was a member of the Royal
Household. Prince Yousef al Saud. One of the many
Royal Princes, Yousef's wealth was from his small oil
field in Jham that netted some one hundred million
dollars a year and his auto dealerships. Any transaction

for an expensive foreign car came through Prince Yousef al Saud. Ferrari's, Lamborghinis, Bentley or a Rolls Royce benefited the Prince. The Central Saudi Construction Partnership was an Al Queda shell company. When matching the names Prince Yousef and Osama bin Laden, they were born in the same year, and were second cousins.

In 1985 there was a purchase made by Prince Yousef for land in the city of Qatif for some two million dollars. In 1986 a Wahabi Temple was built on that site for the cost of five million dollars, then ownership was turned over to the Al Mullah Organization, an Al Queda front. This now was the main religious dogma site for Al Queda and its' troops.

In 1986 the Saudi Construction Partnership purchased equipment from a company in Chechnya called the POZ power group. The transaction was for some eighty million dollars for electrical transformers. POZ was a subsidiary of Mozredh. Mozredh is the biggest arms manufacturer in Russia. Mozredh owners were a listing of Russia's wealthiest billionaires and the number three man in the KGB, a Vladamir Putin.

In 1987 there was a transfer of five million dollars from a Land Rover dealership in Riyadh to Gulf Sea Air Services in Nokomis, Florida. Prince Yousef owned the Land Rover dealership, while Gulf Sea Air was owned by a Eva Corona. A check of Eva Corona, showed her the sole owner and operator of some six seaplanes that serviced the Florida Keys and parts of the Caribbean. Residences for Corona were listed as Nokomis and Banao, Dominican Republic.

Olsen had completed her inquiry and now forwarded the information to Stansfield. He forwarded it to Mike Czarnowski who took a immediate interest in the Nokomis-Banao information. He ordered a surveillance of the Gulf Sea Air Services in Nokomis. Mike then forwarded the rest of the Olsen document to Borush in Tel Aviv, where the new information regarding Prince Yousef and his activities were now given a high priority.

Israeli Military Intelligence was notified to maintain a surveillance of the temple in Qatif. Borush knew that a Wahabi temple did not cost five million to build, unless you were building in extra safeguards, such as munitions storage, which meant deep concrete and steel vaults. The previously unknown activities of Prince Yousef and the new revelation that Ordonez had established a site on US soil were eye openers.

SEVENTY-TWO

1989
Some two months later
Burlington County, NJ Superior Court

THE MURDER CASE against Anthony Conway had lasted 5 weeks. Despite the legal efforts of Conway, Stoddard, and Daniels, the county District Attorney had an open and shut case. Motive was not the issue, they had the gun, the body, the gravesite, and 3 spent shells from Anthony's gun. Over and over the defense tried to play the motive card, but this jury would not listen for the evidence presented was conclusive. The judge could have given the death penalty, but the young Conway would spend the rest of his life in prison. Andrew was devastated. After consulting with Vincent, the appeal would be filed, and Andrew would find out who really killed Tommy Trap. He tried to get in touch with Joshua Devens, but was told he had been transferred to a cutter in the Pacific. What he wanted was the entry logs of the OSE to the Tuckerton channel, but Dan Stansfield already had that information from OSE's Tom Newcomb. Stansfield with the report in his hands found four ships had gotten permission from the Coast Guard to enter the restrictive channel. Of the four, one of them was a marine research vessel from Rutgers. That left three boats entering the channel. The reports from Tom Newcomb indicated that a Seaford International vessel the *Ocean Victory* had arrived for a steering repair at the DelMarVa facility, leaving the next day, two days before the Trap body was found. Another Seaford International vessel the *Augusta Moon* arrived the following day for an anchor hoist repair, leaving the site after nine hours. That left a vessel called the *Carib Palm*, which was experiencing electrical problems. It did not leave until the morning of the third day, the day the search warrant was executed and the body found. Autopsy revealed that Trap was killed that morning. Newcomb did a background on the *Carib Palm*. Owned by a Belgium consortium out of Antwerp, its master was a Guillermo Negras of Barahona, Dominican Republic.

Stansfield,

"Now isn't that a remarkable coincidence. Once again Pedro Ordonez enters into this picture."

He picked up the phone and called Newcomb.

"Tom, can you tell the next port of call for the *Carib Palm*?"

"Genoa, Italy due in on Thursday from Yanbu, Saudi Arabia.

"Thanks Tom."

Stansfield then made a call to Mike Czarnowski in Washington.

"Mike, Dan Stansfield. We just came up with some new developments in our investigation. It seems before Tommy Trap was murdered on the property of DelMar Va Ship and Tool, a ship called the *Carib Palm* was in dock for repairs. It left the morning when the body was discovered. Master of the vessel was a Guillermo Negras, hometown Barahona, Dominican Republic."

Czarnowski,

"Jesus, Ordonez killed Trap?"

"Yes, and made it look like the Conway kid did it."

"Dan, what do you need from me?"

"The *Carib Palm* is due in Genoa on Thursday, can you get it searched?

"I'll get Interpol on it"

CHAPTER SEVENTY-THREE

1990
World Trade Center, NYC

WEARING HIS WHITE hardhat and safety glasses Brian Tynan was a very busy man. He had literally crawled into every crawlspace, basement, sub-basement, and every floor of the World Trade Center Twin towers. With the eye of an engineer, he surveyed out the weak points of the complex. In a few weeks he would take and refine his data that would target the prime location for a bomb to be placed. For the client he was a valuable member of the maintenance support community. Well liked and always available to join a project Brian Tynan was considered a "go to guy" the highest accolade one could have. When he needed anything special, it seemed he could call upon his friends from his Ketchum Park team, the

Banshees. Ten of the team members all worked here in various positions, and if he needed it, no problem. The Friends of Armagh believed he was in New York on a mission for the IRA. Little did they know, his main mission was to recon the target for a future Al Queda attack. He was told by bin Laden to use the American Irish and their money, but make them believe he is here for a British target in mind. Feed them bits and pieces, but never reveal the true target and his findings. With this in mind Tynan knew he would meet McBride at the park and there he would leak out some information. It would be a tightrope to walk, but it was nothing he hadn't done before. On this day he was entering the underground parking garage beneath the North Tower.

Constantly observing the steel beams, he walked each parking level. In the B2 level he saw something that caught his eye. Referring to the blue prints, he always carried, he noticed a huge space in the ceiling that housed a very large aluminum duct measuring approximately 25' wide by 40' long going up to the next level. He found the nearby staircase and went up to the A1 level. This level was about 40 feet below street level. There the duct continued on up to a restaurant on the 3rd floor of the North Tower. He had found the perfect channel for a bomb. Running back down to the B2 level he found a marked space numbered B344 directly in the middle of the ducts span. This was the perfect location for a vehicle packed with high explosive to park. The force would go upward, unhindered, and create a domino effect of collapse. Thousands would die. He wrote down his calculations, and would then start to work up and refine his final presentation.

CHAPTER SEVENTY-FOUR

1990
Genoa, Italy

INTERPOL CHIEF INSPECTOR Phillipe Noire was on the dock as the *Carib Palm* tied up. Accompanying were some 25 officers of the Polizia di Stato (Italian State Police). Noire had a warrant to search the ship, and the power of the State Police to detain the captain and crew indefinitely. Alerted by Mike Czarnowski, he had an additional 10 Interpol Forensic agents carrying portable high intensity UV lights. The captain and crew were removed and escorted off the ship. They all were taken to a small warehouse and under police guard told to make themselves comfortable. The search began with the crew quarters and lockers. Every piece of clothing was examined and placed under the UV light. It was in the engineers quarters they

found a jacket and a pair of pants containing to what
appeared to be blood stains. The jacket belonged to
the chief engineer Marco DiLauri, and the pants belonged to second engineer Pavel Sumerko. The clothing was rushed to Genoa Police Laboratory where it
was found to be human blood Type A positive. The
DNA test took much longer and came back with two
alleles at 14.6 and 13. Noire had the results faxed to
Sean Feeney in New York. Feeney received the fax and
phoned Stansfield and Blackman.

"Right off the press from Phillipe Noire. Type A
positive and alleles at 14.6 and 13."

Blackman checked the lab reports on Trap's blood.

"It is a match! Tell him to make the arrest."

"Will do Red."

Most of the crew were allowed to go. DiLauri and
Sumerko were arrested to be arraigned, and Noire
wanted to question the Captain. After some three
hours, with Negras in isolation the interrogation began in the State Police Questara.

"Captain Negras, I am chief inspector Phillipe
Noire of Interpol. I am here to gather information
regarding our findings during the execution of the
search warrant. Let us go back to your ships stay in
New Jersey at the DelMarVa ship repair dock. What
were you there for?

"We were encountering electrical problems in the

engine room, and I deemed it necessary to pull in for repair."

"How long were those repairs?"

"Three days before we could sail again."

"Were the repairs satisfactory?"

"Apparently we were able to make our next port."

"How much did this repair cost?"

"$100,000 dollars."

"You paid for it?"

"No, it was wired by the consortium of owners in Belgium to DelMarVA before we docked."

"Who are the owners of the *Carib Palm*?"

"I do not know."

"Captain, you do not know who signs your paycheck?"

"I get my money wired into my Genoa bank account, I have no idea who actually pays me. All I know the money is good."

"Where do you call home Captain, Genoa or Barahona?

"While I work, I maintain a residence with my family in Genoa. Barahona is where my uncles and aunts still live."

"Does the name Pedro Ordonez mean anything to you?"

"I do not know the name."

"Does the company called Consuelo Imports mean anything?

'No, never heard of it."

"How well do you know your Chief Engineer Marco Di Lauri?"

"He has been my Chief Engineer for the past five years?

"And Second Engineer Pavel Sumerko?"

"He and DiLauri came on at the same time."

"How long have you been Captain of the *Carib Palm*?

"Five years."

"And before that what vessels were you captain of?"

"My first ship was the Shell Argo which I captained for 2 years, then left for the *Carib Palm*."

"Did you order DiLauri and Sumerko to murder a man in New Jersey?

"I did not.":

"Let me bring you up to date what is happening down the hall. DiLauri and Sumerko are talking. They say you gave them $35,000 each to kill Tommy Trap."

"That is a lie, I did not kill anyone!"

"No, you did not actually kill anyone, you just ordered and paid for it."

"Prove it?"

"We have the victim's blood and DNA match the

bloodstains on DiLauri's jacket and Sumerko's pants. They started talking, and I must say they have been very helpful. It seems they both know Pedro Ordonez and Consuelo Imports because one of the Belgium consortium members is Pedro Ordonez, your wife, Matilda's first cousin. So, Captain Negras it is now time to be honest and forthright, for you are now an accessory to capital murder. Shall we begin?"

SEVENTY-FIVE

1990
Ketchum Park fields, Brooklyn

BRIAN TYNAN MADE a lateral move that left his man flat footed in place. He dribbled then passed the ball perfectly in front of a charging teammate who kicked it in to the left of the sprawling goalie. Banshees 2 Corkers 0. With this win, the Banshees continued in first place, and were in the city playoffs. As Bryan sat on the bench removing his cleats, he felt a hand touch his shoulder.

"Beautiful game Bryan, well played."

He looked up to see Ray McBride smiling."

"Thank you very much."

Ray sat down next to him and said very quietly,

"Brian, me boy can you give us an idea when your device will be finished?

"In another 2 weeks. When it goes off, I will be somewhere else. You just tell me who will pick it up, on what day, and bring my money."

McBride was so elated he patted Bryan again on his shoulder and left.

Martin Callahan could predict what would happen. McBride and his sunshine compatriots would strike a blow for Ireland by attacking some British Institution, causing great damage, but no loss of life. Then they could pound their chests saying they helped the Great Irish Cause. This would appease his supporters, yet nowhere would the shadow of Al Queda be seen. His work was nearly finished at the World Trade Center. He had the data and the prints needed, so all was left was to send it off. There would be no spy tradecraft of marked trees or buried drops, this was very simple, the US Mail. It would all be packaged in a standard mailing envelope and sent to an address in Belgium. In Brussels a nationally known engineering firm would receive it, deliver it to a site trailer, where it would be picked up by a messenger. The messenger would deliver it to the Yemen Embassy, and there by diplomatic pouch would arrive in the capital Sana'a. Another messenger would arrive and pick up the package and deliver it to a house owned by Sheik Mohammed al Suta. The Sheik, war plans and operations minister of Al Queda, would review the data and present it to bin Laden for approval.

Martin Callahan remaining task was to construct a bomb for the Friends of Armagh. It would be similar to the devices he designed that were exploded in London, and Tel Aviv. He cared little about the actual target, he just wanted his money, then he would disappear from America. However, he did know he was the center of an international manhunt.

SEVENTY-SIX

1990
Genoa, Italy

IN THE CONSUELO Import offices, Pedro Ordonez had just received a call from his Al Queda go between, a local meeting was needed. They met at a small café a few blocks away. Bin Laden's emissary was named Bashir Tabiq, a very small man, his eyes darted everywhere. Dressed in western blue jeans and heavy metal t-shirts he looked more like a rock concert roadie than a terrorist.

"Our mutual friend has a message I am to deliver in person, it is of the utmost most importance you listen."

"Go ahead, speak."

"We have learned that there is a very dangerous assassin after you. Your enemy Seaford has paid him to kill you. He found the Filipino Captain Braco in Singapore and killed him."

"Do you know his name or where he is from?"

"All they know, he is based in Sardinia, and his left eye is dark."

"Please thank our mutual friend, I will take the necessary precautions."

Bashir left first, as Pedro placed a phone call.

The call was picked up in Baharona.

"Where is Roberto?

"At his hacienda."

"Get him, and put him on a plane to Genoa to meet me tomorrow."

"Yes jefe."

This news, though unsettling, could not deter Ordonez from his present duties, for today two huge shipments of heroin were arriving in Genoa via another Al Queda recommended supplier. Since Consuelo started doing business with these "recommended sources" his revenues had reached all time highs. The quality of the heroin coming out of the Afghanistan/Taliban controlled fields was of the highest quality, and in turn returned the highest price. The Consuelo ships *Piraeus* and *Andaman Princess* were loaded at the Georgian Black Sea port of Batumi and now were about to dock at the Consuelo terminal in Genoa. Ordonez and his people would now distribute the load to his labs in Marseille, Frankfurt, Brussels, and Oslo for refining. Then final distribution to Europe and the United States networks would follow. For a few seconds his mind drifted to the arrival of his nephew Roberto. The son of his dead brother Jaime, Pedro had made sure the family raised him and that he had a home. At 21, Pedro tried to get him interested in the business, but the boy's mind was elsewhere, so he was turned over to Cousin Eduardo, the family's main enforcer. Roberto killed his first man in Barahona because the man stole from Consuelo. He had the strength and the deadly mind of his late father. To Pedro, he even resembled Jaime, physically and mentally. When Eduardo passed away, Pedro made Roberto the chief enforcer, and soon it was known not to cross Consuelo or the repercussions would be fatal. Pedro would unleash Roberto upon this assassin.

SEVENTY-SEVEN

1990
Brooklyn, NY

THE BOMB WAS packaged in a metal toolbox. Callahan was in the basement of Colleen Murphy's house, and was making sure there were no telltale trails of his work. He heard the doorbell ring, listened to Colleen's footsteps, and heard the shuffling of others in the front foyer. Then the door to the basement opened and Colleen brought down the two visitors downstairs. Callahan in a quick glance saw the two were startled because he had his gun aimed at them. Both raised their hands quickly and one in a high voice said,

"Mr. McBride sent us."

"Do you have my money?"

"Sure, in my coat pocket, can I lower my hands?"

"No, Colleen remove it from his pocket."

Colleen reached in an removed a thick envelope. She handed it to Callahan. He ripped open the envelope and could see it was the right amount.

"Okay, lower your hands. This toolbox is ready to be armed. See this button on the side? Push it in, and then leave the area. It will detonate in 16 minutes. Got that?"

They both said yes. He handed the bigger of the two the toolbox.

"Now leave."

The both left the basement, and he heard the front door close. He then emptied the envelope and counted out $100,000. Turning to Colleen he handed her the money.

"My thanks for making my stay peaceful, let your desires enjoy some of this."

"I will, and may your future journey's be safe. Thank you."

He gathered up the rest of the money, placed it in his pocket. Picked up his travel bag and left Brooklyn forever. The American IRA supporters now were going to make their mark against the British. The two that picked up the bomb, were recruited because they were good supporters, for they talked a good talk when drinking in the bars. They knew how to fight with their fists, and they came from loyal families. All this did not make them experts in planting a bomb.

They were told to go to 355 E. 65th Street and place the bomb in the basement level-parking garage, arm it, then leave. They got into the garage, saw a ledge near a column and placed the toolbox. As the other started up the driveway to the street, the other pressed the button on the side and ran. Getting into their car, they sped down 65th Street and back to Brooklyn. 16 minutes later, the explosion brought down the whole building. When the fire department arrived there was nothing but rubble, rescue operations began. The total body count was fifty four. 37 were children in a nursery school directly above the basement garage, and 17 British Consulate employees. When Ray McBride and Hal Lynch got the news, they raised their glasses and toasted their success. As the news broadcasts came in the death toll of the children was revealed, in shock they put down their glasses and left the bar quickly and unnoticed. The nation was in an uproar over this callous and dastardly attack. The President assured the British Prime Minister all the powers of the United States would find these perpetrators. Three days after the bombing, ATF searchers found the detonating device. Taken to the FBI Lab in Washington, it was an unknown quantity, simple in design, but there was no record of it. The call to Mike Czarnowski came in from Tel Aviv.

"Mike, what's going on with the NY bombing?"

"They found the detonating device, but can't find any record of it. Can't determine the bomb maker if you can't make out the detonator.

"'Can you send me a photo of it, I have some people here who may recognize it"

"Tal give me about 10 minutes, I'll get it out to you."

Czarnowski hung up, and was in touch with the lab.

They sent him an email photo of it, in turn he forwarded it to Borush in Tel Aviv. Five minutes hadn't transpired when his phone rang.

"It was Callahan. He made the bomb. The detonator had a piece of a rubber band hanging from it, it kept a pin against a contact, it was the same as the detonators used by Hezbollah in three Israeli bus bombings. Callahan, has left New York, he got his money. I need to know where he is going, you get me the information that supports it."

"We believe the Friends of Armagh may have paid for this, we have some leads. When we get confirmation you will get a call"

Meantime the powers of the United States government were closing in on Ray McBride and Hal Lynch. McBride was caught at the Mexican border attempting to get to Monterey, and a flight to Algeria. Lynch made it to Canada, and was arrested by Royal Canadian Mounted Police in Halifax, Nova Scotia trying to board a freighter destined for Ireland. Within

hours both were flown to Quantico, Virginia and interrogated. It was once said the true patriot will give
up his life for his cause, while the sunshine patriot will
seek a different cause to save his life. They both gave
up Bryan Tynan and Colleen Murphy.

FBI agents and the NYPD Emergency Services
Squad hit Colleen Murphy's home on a Sunday
morning.

She was the toughest one to crack for she was a true
zealot, the reason to hate had come to her violently and
had fused her soul. The interrogators got nothing from
her. It was here that the medical technicians entered.
Bound by straps to a chair they started the drug
regimen. She tried to fight it, but her inner firewalls
were breached, she became delirious, but they were
able to bring her out of it and continue their relentless
questioning. Where was he going? What part of the
world did he want to live in? On the third day they
finally hit pay dirt. She remembered a supper they had
shared, both were a little high on their second bottle
of wine, when Tynan said he would never return to
Ireland, he had found peace by the ocean. Where was
this place? They kept asking when she blurted out the
name of the place,

"Al Mukalla."

"Where is Al Mukalla, tell us?"

She started shaking, then her eyeballs rolled back.

She went into shock, and had stopped breathing. Quickly disconnecting the straps, they placed her on the floor and tried to use a AED device, but Colleen Murphy never recovered. Another martyr for the cause was claimed. Mike Czarnowski got the information from the interrogators, and immediately called Borush.

"We got the place Callahan may be trying to get to, does Al Mukalla mean anything to you?"

"Yes, it is on the Gulf of Aden in Yemen."

"Can you get him? If we try, it will take weeks. Tal make it happen."

"My teams will be briefed and away within the next twelve hours. We will try and bring him back alive, but there are no guarantees when dealing with an Al Queda operative."

"I fully understand, and shalom"

"Shalom to you Mike."

SEVENTY-EIGHT

1990
Cagliari-Elmas Airport, Sardinia

W ITH THE PRECISE instructions of his uncle, Roberto
Ordonez retrieved his baggage and hailed a cab
for the 7km ride to Cagliari. At the Brezza Marina
Hotel, a room was reserved for Ceasare DiNobli, a
businessman from Naples. He made a local phone call
to a number provided by his uncle.

"Cagliari Port office."

"May I speak with Enzo Nini?"

After a few minutes,

"This is Enzo."

"My name is Ceasare DiNobli, our mutual friend
at Consulelo Shipping told me to call you."

"Yes, I was told you would call. It would be best if
we meet in a public place."

"Your choice."

"In an hour, the outdoor café called Bocolla, across from the post office on Via Dela Paneta. I will be wearing a Barcelona FC shirt."

"I will find you."

In an hour, Roberto found the man in the football shirt.

He went over and sat down. Extending his hand he said.

"Ceasare DiNobli"

"Enzo Nini, it is a pleasure. `How may I be of service?"

I need to secure the services of an assassin. A family matter requires that this be immediate. Money is no object, with one request."

"What is that request?"

"I personally meet the assassin, so I can see his eyes, I want to be sure I have hired the right man."

"I will asked some sources of mine who comes highly recommended. Can I contact you at your hotel? This may take a day to set up a meeting. Where are you staying ?"

"The Brezza Marina."

"I will be in touch." Then Nini got up an left.

Roberto left some fifteen minutes later, unaware he was being tailed.

The next day he received a call from Nini to be in

front of his hotel at noon, a taxicab with the number 5778 will pick him up. Roberto, strapped a knife to the inside of his leg, and a small pistol in his inside pocket. A noon he left the hotel and got into cab 5778. What seemed like 15 minutes, the cab stopped at a apartment house off the main road of Cagliari. He was told to go to the third floor, apartment 3F. No elevator was available, so he walked up the dark stairway. Reaching the third floor. He knocked on door 3F. Opened by a young woman in her twenties, she told him to come in and sit in the kitchen. About a minute later, an older man in his fifties came in and sat.

"You need a specific person with skills to do a job? Where may I ask?"

"Naples, at my home. I want my wife killed."

The man looked at him at him face to face. That was when Roberto saw the dark left eye. He reached for his pistol and aimed at the man. Just then a shot rang out, and he was hit in his right hand dropping the gun to the floor. With his left he reached for his knife, but the young girl fired again and hit his left hand. He got up to grab the older man by his neck, then he was knocked unconscious, someone had hit him from behind. Three men came into the kitchen, and rolled Roberto up in a rug and carried it outside to a van. The van travelled some fifty miles to the East Coast of Sardinia. Climbing to an altitude 1000 feet up a mountain, they brought the still unconscious Roberto to a large room. He was bound hand and feet to a chair. An hour later he started to awake. As he looked up there was another older man, dressed in an expensive suit and tie. His left eye bore also the birthmark.

"Ah, welcome to Castille Sassari, Mr. Roberto Ordonez, I believe I am the man you were sent to kill?

"Who was the man in the apartment?

"My twin brother, who makes sure I am protected at all costs."

"How do you know my real name."

"It was expected, your Uncle Pedro would respond by sending his family enforcer. I make it my business to know everything about my targets. I was hired by a client to kill your uncle. He sent you, and I assume there will be more coming. So I will wait and dispose of his minions one by one. Then when the time is right, your Uncle will die. Roberto, I cannot say it was a pleasure meeting you, but your Uncle has wasted your time and talents on a useless errand. Take him to the Grotto." Roberto was released from his constraints, handcuffed behind his back, and marched out of the room by three men. Outside the castle he could see the ocean and the sea birds. As they came to a terrace, one of the men opened a gate. He felt a large chain being attached to his handcuffs, Attached to the chain were four cinder blocks. Then he felt a push, then the speed of flight downward. He fell some 400 feet and hit the water. The attached blocks brought him downward to a depth of some 300 feet. The Grotto had taken another victim, as it had for centuries prior.

CHAPTER SEVENTY-NINE

1990
Haifa, Israel

SAYERET 7 WAS to be the scout force. They would find and surround the target. Comprising the best Israeli Defense Forces soldiers, they formed one of the world's best special force units. Eight operators acted as one. Fast and stealthy they would penetrate the target area, relay information and for this mission provide external security. The killing team was made up of four Mossad agents or kidons. Highly trained in the facets of assassination and kidnapping their part was to find the target, and in this case bring him back alive. If the target resisted, they would kill him in the bat of an eye.

Getting to Yemen was the easy part, the IDF submarine Satila would get them to within 1000 yards of the Yemen coast. It would take about day and a half

to get to the area off of Al Mekalla, so Borush made
arrangements for the sub to carry two RQ2 Pioneer
drones. They could be launched at night from the deck
of the sub and sent over Al Mekalla sending back
videos. The duration of each drone over target was 8
hours, with two drones you would get continuance
of coverage. On the eve of the second day the Satila
surfaced about a mile off the target. The first rubber
raft was launched with the Sayeret, who would make
landfall an hour before the Kidon. The sub crew would
launch the Pioneer; with its Infrared cameras every
building would be scanned. Once the building hous-
ing Callahan was verified, the Sayeret would surround
it. The raft containing the Kidon was launched. The
Sayeret reported that they had found a good hide,
until the target was spotted. As the drone flew some
10,000 feet above Al Mekalla, the operators on board
the sub, noticed that most of the village huts were
small and were crudely constructed, while about a
mile from village center was a piece of property with a
substantial house. A swimming pool, and a new model
Land Rover parked out front. An attached dock and
boathouse on the beach completed the property. The
Infrared picked up 3 bodies located outside the house
all carrying weapons. It was quickly determined this
was Callahan's lair. The Sayeret were sent to the surround the area, and take out the sentries.

The Kidon were to arrive 20 minutes later and breach the house. As this was taking place, Martin Callahan was in bed with his girlfriend of 10 years, Katherine Lavall, a French fashion model. They had met in Lyon, and their relationship blossomed. Both never wanted to marry, but considered each other their lifetime mate. She waited for him while he travelled the world, he would keep up with her, by seeing her photographs in the fashion magazines. They had long planned a home in a desolated area, and the house and property were their dream fulfilled. They had sex that night, and as she laid on the bed, she smiled at his snoring. Now united with her lover and friend she was happy. The hand over her mouth and the needle into her neck came so fast she was unable to react. Callahan was slowly awakened by an itch on his nose. As he opened his eyes there was a dark figure holding a pistol. The needle put him back to sleep. The entire mission was over within 25 minutes. Martin Callahan was loaded into the raft, while the woman was left in her bed. Both teams made it back to the Satila. The operators radioed back to Haifa, that the "four leaf clover" is on the way. Martin Callahan now had a date with some very anxious people in British MI-6.

 CHAPTER **EIGHTY**

1990
Bass River Station

A DAY HAD GONE by when the group was notified that Al Queda's bomb maker had been captured. In the conference room were Sharon Olsen,
Red Blackman, Sean Feeney, Mike Czarnowski and
Dan Stansfield.

As always, Stansfield chaired the meetings.

"With the apprehension of the bomb maker, we
may get some more information on Consuelo, so
where do we stand?

Feeney,

"This case from the beginning has been a tilting
match between Consuelo and New Seaford. We cannot predict the next incident because we have no inside
intelligence."

Blackman,

"To get that intelligence we need to find a source that will tell us what one side or the other is doing, and we cannot come up with that source."

Czarnowski,

"I have confirmed that there is very little intelligence on either Consuelo or New Seaford. This group has the most gathered to date."

It was then that Sharon Olsen spoke.

"During my laboratory days, whenever we got stumped at a crime scene, the veteran guys would always say,

….."stop what your doing, relax, and think outside the box".… It worked every time for we uncovered more evidence that solved the case. What we need to do with this case is think outside the box or push that envelope till it is about to burst."

Stansfield,

"In other words change to another course to solve the crime?

"Yes, do something you normally would not do, so as to gain a new perspective, but staying within the rules."

Czarnowski,

"The US Attorneys of the DOJ call it Queen for a Day.

Bring in a secondary person of interest, sit him

down and tell him he will be indicted and go to prison, but if he co-operates with them fully during the next 12 hours, no charges will be issued, but it must be the truth. Any lies and the deal's null and void. It is a great tool to eventually get the number one guy."

Feeney,

"So tell me who do we deal with in this case?"

Not much comment from the group, but Blackman was flipping thru the casebook, he knew with all the interviews there was someone who could flip, if the carrot was big enough. Then he punched the table with his fist hollering,

"Son of a bitch!

All at the table were silent except for Feeney, for he had seen this many times.

"Bagels found the answer."

EIGHTY-ONE

1990
New Seaford Headquarters

A S ANDREW CONWAY was about to sip his morning cup of coffee, his phone rang. It was Vincent Conway.

"Hello Vincent."

"Andrew, I just got an odd phone call. He would not identify himself, but said for me to be at the Bass River State Police barracks in half an hour."

Andrew could not fathom what this was about, until he heard commotion outside his office door. He opened it to find a uniformed state trooper.

"Are you Andrew Conway?

"This is a search warrant for these premises signed by Judge Walter Rollins of the 7ᵗʰ NJ Superior Court. You will please step out of your office, and you and your employees leave the premises." Andrew went back to his desk, picked up his phone and said,

"Vincent, they are executing a search warrant of my office, why?

"I don't know but comply, or it will get worse."

Vincent hung up and Andrew got his suit jacket and left for the exit. As he was about to enter his car, Stansfield came over to him, identified himself and said.

"Andrew, it may be wise for you to follow me to the Bass River barracks. Your choice."

Andrew thought for a few seconds, smiled, then said,

"I believe my attorney is enroute."

"Yes, he is, I did not want to delay this matter anymore."

"Well, Trooper Stansfield, I guess I am following you."

It took about 25 minutes when they reached the barracks. Conway was shown a seat in the conference room. About 10 minutes later Vincent Conway arrived, and was also shown a seat in the conference room. Stansfield and team awaited outside, then they all walked in and sat opposite the Conway's.

Stansfield,

I would like to thank you both for coming here. I am the lead investigator on the murders of your relatives Patrick and Timothy Blaine. To my immediate left are Detective Lt. Sean Feeney of the NYPD, and retired Detective Captain Morris Blackman of the NYPD. Both of these men were the lead investigators for the murder of one Vincent Conway, Jr. To my right is Mrs. Sharon Olsen, a Forensic Genealogist who has worked with the NYPD on several high profile cases. Special Agent Michael Czarnowski of the FBI, Washington, DC. rounds out our team.

First, allow me to acquaint you with the facts we have acquired to date with this co-investigation.

A. Vincent Conway Jr was murdered during a drug buy in the Bronx. He shot and killed one Ramon Ordonez before he was killed by multiple gunshots. Vincent was found in the trunk of his company car that was underwater in the East River. Attempts to preliminary investigate this case by searching his apartment proved difficult in that his apartment was swept by unidentified persons. The only line of evidence we found a parking ticket for illegally parking in a driveway that happened to be your companies former warehouse in Brooklyn. Then we have a military style operation that was perpetrated on the drug site where Vincent Conway Jr. was killed. The entire drug gang was massacred, yet no one responsible has been charged. The

opinion of this group is that this was the start
of the Consuelo/New Seaford war.

B. Patrick and Timothy Blaine were both murdered
on the same day. They were smuggling in cocaine
using a cigarette boat. Hijacked at sea by another
boat and a helicopter, Patrick was shot dead and
thrown overboard. Timothy was wounded and
hoisted to the helicopter. The boat and its cargo
were taken somewhere and unloaded, and the
boat left in Ocean City, Maryland. Timothy,
mortally wounded somehow fell from the helicopter and died upon impact on the grounds of
a pharmaceutical plant in Dorothy, NJ.

C. All the victims had the same tattoo on their
inner right arm, a oval surrounding an anchor,
which we believe to be a indication of devotion
and duty within the family. It appears all males
be it Conway, Thompson or Blaine have this
same tattoo. My guess is both you two gentle-
men have this same tattoo, but that is not any
interest of ours at this time.

D. We do know that you laundered money thru
your Cayman Island accounts with the late
Tommy Trap.

E. We have reason to believe that the murder of
Arturo Bracos in Singapore was ordered by you,
Andrew Conway.

F. We have evidence that you, Andrew Conway did enter a top secret government facility thru your relationship with one Joshua Devins. This is a Federal offense of the Department of Defense protocols.

And that is what we have accumulated so far".

Vincent Conway,

"Detective Stansfield my client and I appreciate all your teams work, but you have nothing that involves my client in any of this. So why was my client subject to a search warrant?

Mike Czarnowski,

"To get him away from his comfort zone and bring him here, because we have more for you to hear."

"Please continue, we will hear you out.

"I have been working with several foreign law enforcement and intelligence agencies on international terrorism. We learned that Consuelo Imports made a deal with a radical Muslim organization to transport their operatives into Europe and the U.S.. In return Consuelo gets to distribute cocaine, and entry to the heroin suppliers of Afghanistan. Pedro Ordonez, CEO of Consuelo Imports, and a surviving brother of the family that killed Vincent Conway Jr. has been waging war against your client. That same family that was massacred in the Bronx, has a reason to hate the New Seaford Corporation. We believe he set fire to your

Brooklyn warehouse, and hijacked Seaford's boats the *Abigail Conway* and the *Tiger Star.* We believe they were refurbished and disguised for use by Consuelo Imports. Most recently a man by the name of Martin Callahan was brought illegally into the United States by a Consuelo Import ship. For the last few months he worked in New York City as a building engineer. His real job was in Yemen as the chief bomb maker for a radical Muslim organization. He constructed a bomb for IRA American supporters, then left the country. That bomb killed the 37 children and 17 adults at the British Consulate in New York. Callahan was apprehended and returned to the United Kingdom for judgment. We want Pedro Ordonez, and you will help us."

Vincent Conway,

"Agent Czarnowski, my client has no inkling of this Pedro Ordonez, I am sorry but my client cannot help you."

Both Conway's got up to leave, when Red Blackman spoke up,

"Gentleman, Consuelo and Ordonez murdered your relatives, and now they pose a threat to our country surely you must realize he must be caught and brought to justice."

Andrew Conway,

"Not any of my business."

Feeney,

"What will make it your business Andrew?"

"Look, do not bring up service to my country, I did that already. My only responsibility is to my clan, and to make New Seaford profitable every year. I knew who Ordonez was way before I walked into this room, and if I have to confront him, it we be on my terms and my terms alone.. Your proposing I bring him to you because he poses a threat to the country, well I learned some time ago from my father and his father that when a larger entity comes to a smaller entity, disaster will befall the smaller. New Seaford co-operates with no one. I do not need you."

Blackman,

"Your right Andrew, you do not have to help your country, and you can take care of Ordonez on your own. You and cousin Vincent can walk out of here and laugh this whole thing off. Go ahead, you're free to walk out of here, but I know we can be of service to you for something you personally cannot accomplish."

Andrew Conway,

"And what may that be?"

"The release of your son Anthony."

Andrew Conway smile left his face, and he was speechless.

Vincent Conway,

"Are you trying to blackmail my client? If you are, I will report this, I am an officer of the court."

Blackman,

"Vincent, blackmail is not on this table, just a sug-
gestion that Andrew reconsider his stance, and see the
benefit."

The two Conways' started whispering to each
other. You could see there was disagreement, but they
stopped and Vincent Conway spoke.

"If my client agrees to help you, what?"

Czarnowski,

"The capture of Pedro Ordonez, alive. Seaford is
his mortal enemy. He will never stop at a chance to
hurt you and your family. You get us Ordonez inside
the borders of the United States and he will be arrested
for all he has done."

Andrew Conway.

"So you're using me as bait?"

Blackman,

"Plain and simple Andrew, yes. You give him to
us, Anthony is released, no record of his conviction,
no prison time, a clean sheet."

Andrew looked straight a Blackman,

"You thought this up, didn't you? Using my son to
get me in, you're a smart son of a bitch. If my son is
not released, you're the first on my list."

Blackman,

"Andrew prepare to get in line, I'm number one on
lists more important than yours. You are a thief, born

and bred. I saw what your capable of, and it didn't
scare me. I was a cop once, now retired, but never
forgetting the cases that still bother me. Brown Place
was the key to the Vincent Conway Jr. murder, and
you came in like the great avenger, destroying everything. My partner and I wanted to pursue you, but the
politicians thought you did a community service. No
Andrew, I could give a rat's ass about your kid either
way. Ordonez is more important than you, and right
now he is the one we want. Don't come on board, well
that would be a bad decision for a man who makes
important decisions everyday regarding his family and
their interests. We will eventually get Pedro, may take
a little longer than we have planned, but we will get
him. The persons in this room now know you, and
your operations. We will become your new nightmare.
Do you think we will forget about New Seaford if you
do not co-operate?

Andrew face had changed color, he looked a Vincent
Conway, they whispered for about two minutes.

Vincent Conway,

"My client will render his assistance, and the release of Anthony Conway will be implemented upon
the seizure and arrest of Pedro Ordonez. Are we in
agreement.?"

Stansfield.

"Yes Mr. Conway, we are in agreement. We will

be in touch with your client within the week. Can we provide transportation back to Fire Road?"

"No that will not be necessary, I will provide transportation for my client."

Both Conway's got up and left. Feeney smiled at Sharon Olsen and quietly said,

"That was Bagels at his best."

CHAPTER EIGHTY-TWO

1990
Haifa, Isreal
Airport Ramp 12 East

A T 2AM MARTIN Callahan, under a black hood was
walked up the stairs and cuffed to the seat. Tal
Borush shook hands with Neville Crofts of MI-6.

"Thank you Tal, we will proceed with the next
stage. We know what Mossad wants, and we will get
him to talk."

"Neville, we all need to know about bin Laden and
his future plans, this guy must know."

"Let's hope we can find that out."

They shook hands and Borush left the interior of
the jet.

Within minutes the RAF A330MRTT was air-
borne with one very important passenger, surrounded

by 8 armed SAS troopers. Seven hours later the jet landed at Brize North Royal Air Force Base, UK. Quickly exiting the plane he was place aboard an adjacent aircraft a Hawker 1000 MI-6 jet that immediately took off and flew north. Never seeing where he was, Martin Callahan, realized this was the probably the last airplane ride of this odyssey. Three hours later, they landed on the Isle of Unst. Unst, the northernmost Shetland Islands, was barren and forbidding. The site of a former Royal Army Test Facility would be Callahan's interrogation. Placed in a cell, his hood was removed. He expected exactly his surroundings. A bed with one blanket, a single light bulb some 12 feet up, a toilet and no window. An hour went by when two guards brought him food and drink. The food was tolerable, and the tea was soothing. He wanted to go to sleep, but they came for him. Taken from the cell to a room, his arms and legs were strapped to a chair. A set of headphones was placed on his head, goggles painted black over his eyes, and his neck was duct taped to the back of the chair. He could not move.

A voice came thru the earphones,

"Callahan, you are now in the custody of MI-6. You need not know where you are, but you will later be asked questions regarding your work. Meanwhile, do think about cooperating, as you listen to the souls that you killed. His eyes widened instantly as high-pitched human screams, moans and explosions racked his ears. The next 3 hours he listened to this collection of sounds. His inner ear started to ache. After another 2 hours he vomited and passed out. Waking up he was back in his cell. They came for him again, and sat him down handcuffed to a table. A man entered the room, he was holding a folder, he sat down across from Callahan.

Opening the folder he silently went over the enclosed papers. Then he looked up and said.

"Tell me about Pedro Ordonez?"

"Never heard of him."

The man got up, closed the folder, and walked out,

Seconds later Callahan was back strapped to the chair with the goggles and earphones for a six-hour session.

He again passed out in the chair, and again came to.

Unstrapped from the chair he was stood up and handcuffed and brought back into the interrogation room. The same man carrying the folder came in and asked him the same question. This time he did not answer, and again the man stood up and left the room.

As before he was taken out of the interrogation and hookup to the loud sounds while strapped to the chair.

He passed out after 2 hours, but when he woke up, he was still in the chair, and the sounds were still going.

It took an hour for him to pass out, then he was returned to the interrogation room.

"Tell me about Pedro Ordonez?"

Callahan could not speak or form the words in his mouth. The interrogator viewed this as silence and got up to leave. Callahan pounded the desk and kept nodding yes. They brought in some tea and sandwiches. His voice starting to return, and he was asked the same question again.

Callahan

"He is the main transporter for Osama bin Laden's operation.

"Where did you meet him?"

"In the Dominican Republic, I was his guest overnight.

The mission was to get me into the US."

"What name did you use?"

"Malcolm McGuiness."

"What was your mission?"

'To meet with and build a device for the Friends of Armagh."

"And that was the device that exploded at the British Consulate in New York City?"

"Yes."

"Were you paid?"

"Yes."

"How much?"

"$500,000."

"Tell me the names of the persons who paid you for the job?"

"Ray McBride and Hal Lynch."

"Did you work in New York?"

"Yes, they got me a job in Manhattan. I was a HVAC engineer for Lynch's company."

"What name did you use?"

"Freddie Donnely."

"Who is Colleen Murphy?"

"An Irish patriot."

"You stayed at her home, while in NYC?"

"Yes."

"Why did bin Laden send you to New York?"

"He owed the IRA for their assistance in a bombing."

"Did you place the bomb in the underground parking area of the British Consulate?"

"No, two sunshine patriots from McBride came to Brooklyn with my money. I gave them the bomb and left New York that day."

"Tell me how you got back to Yemen?"

"I called Ordonez from Miami, he personally came in a seaplane and picked me up. Flew out to sea, landed near one of his ships. I got on the ship and was in Yanbu, Saudi Arabia within 9 days sailing. Got a private flight back to my home in Yemen."

"Was Ordonez in the plane that landed in Miami."

"Yes, he was the pilot."

"We have you as the bomb maker for some 30 incidents in Belfast, 18 in London, and 3 in Israel, and now NYC, am I correct?"

'The ones in Israel were of my design, but assembled by Hezbollah. Osama advised me to do it that way."

"What are the future plans of Osama bin Laden?"

"To rid the Muslim world of western influence, and wage a holy war."

"Do you know where he will strike next?"

"Not a clue, I am given a lot of money, a beautiful place to live, and all the women I want. No, I have no idea of the inner workings of Al Queda."

"You will remain here until we are told to move you. You will face a military trial in Great Britain, that is all for now."

The interrogator left the room, to send his findings to the London office. Callahan thought about his future as he awaited the transfer back to his cell. He had told the Brits some truths, and some he lied about. Never said anything about his real mission in New York or the name he used. Let them try me in a military court, the news will get out, and the cause will protest loudly. He knew the verdict was already in, but he would play their game and waste time so Al

Queda can mount another attack. Be patient he said to himself.

When the interrogation report was transmitted to London, Neville Crofts went through its entirety, briefed his superiors, then called Tal Borush and Mike Czarnowski. They were told the entire report, and copies would be hand delivered to them by MI-6 couriers.

# CHAPTER EIGHTY-THREE

1991
Bass River State Police Barracks

IT HAD BEEN four weeks since they had met with
Andrew Conway, it was now after New Years and
Stansfield began to wonder about Conway's agreement.

Red Blackman was having a cup coffee going over
the shipping reports regarding Consuelo.

"Hey Red, this is taking longer than I wanted it to,
is Conway going to call?"

"He'll call, his son going free cannot be turned
down."

Stansfield's phone rang, he picked it up and heard
the voice of Vincent Conway.

"Detective, my client will meet with Mr. Blackman
only. Please inform him to be at the New Seaford

Corporate offices at 11:30 am on Wednesday. We will discuss the arrangements agreed upon."

Conway hung up. Stansfield looked at Blackman.

"You called it Red, it's on for tomorrow at 11:30 in the morning at New Seaford. He will only talk to you. Do you want to go in wired?"

"No, we are going to have show trust with Andrew, if he thinks were not on the level, he'll throw me out."

The next day Blackman arrived at the Seaford headquarters on time. He was shown into a small conference room and took a chair. About two minutes later Andrew Conway came in and sat down.

Blackman,

"Where's your lawyer?"

"What we have to discuss, he does not want to know.

So let's begin.

Blackman,

"In order for us to arrest Ordonez, we have to catch him in the act, and within the U.S. borders. We need to present him with something so tantalizing, he cannot resist showing up. Can you provide the bait?"

"I can do that."

"What do you have in mind?"

"$60 million in gold bullion, $35 million in Platinum bars, and $100 million in cut diamonds."

"What is the destination."

"San Juan, Puerto Rico on the 21st of this month, Pier 71. That will be the place he will show up. There is no negotiation on this next point. Upon Vincent's approval of Anthony's release agreement have been met, you will release my son to Vincent's custody at 1PM on the 21st.

"Agreed."

"The "bait" belongs to me, you will not confiscate it, is that clear?"

"Agreed."

"You can expect, Ordonez and his people to be on the pier at dusk. Then you can grab him. I will not be in the area, but my people will be watching."

"We only want Pedro Ordonez, you provide the bait, we bag him our deal is over."

"And I nor my family will no longer be of any future interest to your group?"

"That's the agreement."

"Ok, we're finished here, my secretary will show you the way out."

Blackman drove back to Bass River and reported the plan to Stansfield.

"I'll call Mike, and get him up to date. He'll be pissed we can't grab Conway's contraband, but in getting Ordonez it will be worth it. Did Conway ever ask about why we offered up his son?"

"No, never asked. He thinks he got over on us, so

I'm never go to tell him we have two Interpol confessions and supporting DNA evidence that his kid never killed Tommy Trap. Let him believe he pulled this all off. One thing for sure, he will never forget us, he'll not want to arouse our interest."

CHAPTER EIGHTY-THREE

1991
San Juan, Puerto Rico
Harbor, May 21st

THE FBI SURVEILLANCE Team noted the landing of the De Havilland Twin Otter seaplane bearing Dominican Republic markings. Photos were taken of the pilot as he stepped down from the tied up aircraft. He was escorted to a black sedan. Followed by the team to a large mansion located in the area of Isla Verde, he remained there till 12 PM, when the black sedan was on the move again. At 1230 he was in a harbor warehouse area meeting with 2 trucks of men. Weaponry was observed being past amongst this assemblage. Word was sent that Pedro Ordonez had been identified as the pilot of the seaplane and the person in the black sedan. He was now standing in the middle of this group of heavily armed men. A call was placed to Rahway State Prison and Anthony Conway was released into the custody of Vincent Conway. For the next five hours Ordonez and his people waited for sundown. At 6:50 PM truck engines were started and left for Pier 71. The New Seaford ship *Ocean Victory* was tied to the pier. A single engineer mate stood watch in the engine room. The ship had been unloaded four hours before and cleared by Customs. The two trucks arrived, and Pedro Ordonez got out of the lead vehicle. He directed two man to the engine room to tie up the mate. The rest of his armed gang gathered around the area of hidden Hold #5. Pedro was on the bridge and opened the panel that controlled the secret hold. The hold opened and there was nothing in it. Lights came on from all directions, a bullhorn was heard,

"This is the FBI, drop your weapons, and raise your hands!"

One of the men fired his weapon at a light. An FBI sniper shot him thru the head some 400 meters away.

Immediately, weapons were dropped, and a flurry of armed agents came on board. Pedro Ordonez tried to escape but was stopped by Mike Czarnowski aiming a AR-15 at his stomach. Handcuffed, Pedro was taken separately to the U.S. Naval Air Station, San Juan and flown off in a C-130 to Quantico, Virginia. There he was formally charged before a U.S. Magistrate, and placed in a solitary cell in the Marine brig. In days to come, Pedro was interrogated in regard to his dealings with Osama bin Laden, then indicted for international terrorism and murder. His trial was short and without any publicity. Sentenced to 80 years, he was sent to the Super-Max Federal prison in Stanley, North Dakota.

Blackman, Feeney, Olsen and Stansfield celebrated the closings of their cases with a bottle of Bushmills Irish whiskey. Talking about the case, Feeney asked.

"Did Mikey ever find out why the ship was empty?"

"No, he never said, but I checked with my buddy at OSE.

The *Ocean Victory* had been in the Black Sea port of Soschi taking on cargo. She left on May 5th and arrived on the 21st in San Juan."

"Did she stop anywhere else?

"No, satellite surveillance showed her non–stop all the way."

Blackman,

"Then how did she show up empty?"

"Because Andrew Conway had his other ship the *Augusta Moon* in St. Petersburg loaded on the 4th, and arriving in Baltimore on the 20th. He had no intention of losing that load from the start."

All the glasses were refilled, and a toast was offered, "To William Conway the last honest Conway."

POST SCRIPTS

June 3, 1992, U.S Penitentiary, Stanley, North Dakota

Prisoner #457996 was holding his food tray when the stiletto entered his back. His spinal column was severed and Pedro Ordonez pitched forward. Immediately held up by the prisoners next to him, he was guided over a table and seated. A prisoner came over and sat down facing him. Pedro could not speak as the man spoke.

"For threatening the Sassari, you have paid the price."

He could not answer, the room was spinning, he was losing his vision, then total silence.

February 23, 1993 New York City

Eyad Ismoil and Ramzi Yousef drove the rented van into the garage of World Trade Center North Tower stopping on the B level. Driving slowly they looked for space B344. Finding a car parked in that space they found an empty space at B339. Parking the van, Ismoil then lit a 20 foot long fuse and both men ran out of the garage. Minutes later the van and its contents exploded resulting in six dead and over a 1000 injured. If they had waited for the car to leave space B344, and followed Al Queda's recommendation, they would have killed thousands more and most likely have toppled the North Tower. Fate that day favored the innocent.

THE END

Printed in the United States
By Bookmasters